Winter Garden

WINTER GARDEN
Robert Edric

ANDRE DEUTSCH

First published 1985 by
André Deutsch Limited
105 Great Russell Street London WC1B 3LJ

British Library Cataloguing in Publication Data

Edric, Robert
   Winter garden.
   I. Title
   823'.914[F]   PR6055.D7
   ISBN 0–233–97756–2

Typeset by Inforum Ltd, Portsmouth
Printed in Great Britain by
Ebenezer Baylis and Son Ltd, Worcester

For Sara

Christmas Day

The girl's body has been removed. All that remains is a staked outline of tight string and wooden pegs. A circle of men squat around the shape and point with their pens to its angles, already guessing at what they might mean. A simple polythene shelter has been erected over the site, heavy cables trailing to mesh-covered lights hanging from above. The soil skirting the structure has been trodden to mud and all the policemen wear wellingtons, walk cautiously, and complain at the conditions. The girl's outline remains as distinct against the dark soil as a chalk horse against a green hillside. This will not last.

The allotments have been closed, and a fifty-yard radius of where the body was found has also been staked and roped. This area is guarded by six constables who stamp their feet and blow into their hands.

Vehicles line the road leading from the allotments into town. Police cars sit with their doors open, radios crackling and drivers with their dirty feet still on the road. In a waiting ambulance the driver reads yesterday's paper and his mate stares through the windscreen, drumming his fingers on the dashboard and speculating about the body and what has happened.

Below, in the town, a dozen churches celebrate the birth of Christ, their bells interlocking, rising and fading, disguising any single rhythm of peals.

The lights above the polythene shelter have been on all night, shining white over the frozen soil, leaving the police guards like ghosts in their capes, and casting sharp antiseptic shadows over the bare ground.

Now, at ten in the morning, a line of men move methodically across the roped area, probing the ground with slender canes, ignoring the radios which come to life on their lapels. Across the allotments a whistle sounds and the muted barking of excited dogs can be heard.

The soil and refuse under which the girl's body had been hidden is being carefully removed by men wearing rubber gloves who carry it in sacks to the rear of a waiting van. They stand in a

3

group, talking and smoking, and watching the onlookers who line the police cordon and refuse to be dispersed.

In the tent-like structure itself stand three men. They have examined the body and considered their chances of finding anything of value on the surrounding land, cursing the fact that anything which might have helped them will almost certainly have been destroyed by the allotment owners. The doctor estimates the body to be eight weeks old, possibly ten. He says it is difficult to be accurate because of the effects of the low temperatures, of the frost and the constant thawing and re-freezing of the ground.

The men leave the cramped interior and stand outside, filling the cold air with plumes of blue smoke. They discuss again their chances of finding anything which might point them towards the killer and shake their heads. To their juniors and the lower ranks they shout confidently, stirring up enthusiasm.

In addition to the cold and the allotment owners, the detectives curse the fact that it is Christmas, and that certain procedures are less likely to be undertaken as quickly as they might otherwise have been. They turn to watch two constables who shout and wave their arms to scare away the flocks of seagulls and crows which constantly scavenge over the land. One of the detectives makes a note of the birds in his pocket book. Another mentions that the gulls will eat anything and that their presence ought to be pointed out to whoever performs the medical examination of the body. The others screw up their faces at the thought and turn to watch the birds and listen to their cries.

By four in the afternoon it is dark, and the headlights of the waiting cars shine yellow over the ground, picking out the few men who remain. The brightly illuminated shelter stands ringed with darkness. The silhouette of a man moves around inside. Below the site, beads of light map out the shape of the town, a dark void indicating the sea. Away to the left swings the beam of the lighthouse, running over the deserted caravan sites and the cold, empty spaces beyond.

The red, yellow and blue outline of the Spa Theatre is clearly visible, its giant illuminations of a grinning clown and parrot recognisable even at that distance.

In ten thousand homes, ten thousand Christmases are being celebrated. On the hill, at the centre of the dark allotments, stands the illuminated shelter from which the girl's body has

4

been removed, looking for all the world like a giant, ornamental crib, surrounded by the lights and sounds of the men come to celebrate its meaning.

November

I

The gulls hung above the water, rising and falling against the pushing wind like toys on elastic cords. Beneath the surface, the sewage outlet gushed its warm waste, heating the water, discolouring it, and giving it the faintly sickly aroma which attracted the birds.

On the exposed and deserted beach a solitary man threw a ball for his dog and turned his back to the wind. He shouted to the dog and watched the surface patterns of the skimming sand as it collected against the groynes. Further along the beach stood the concrete stumps of wartime tank traps which had trapped no tanks, and which now sank beneath the soft sand, dragged out of line by the sea. Besides the man's voice there was only the sound of the gulls, an echo of children in a playground. He stood and listened, and the dog raced ahead of him.

Parallel to the beach ran the South Shore Promenade, along which the more imposing hotels jostled for position, staking their claims to the sea views afforded by the site. Now there was little to see but the sea and the sky, merged in a single darkness, and the gulls which continued in clumsy circles.

Roads ran at right angles from the Promenade into the wet and dormant heart of the out-of-season town.

It was Sunday. It had been raining for most of the day and the streets shone, reflecting the lines of street lights which made them appear narrower than they were. Along these dark streets the rain threatened sleet, and in less than a month there would be a weak fall of snow. In window after window, Vacancy signs hung like hopeless dreams. From behind them came the orange glow of fireside lamps, televisions and fires.

Norman sat on the floor beside the gas fire. Alice, whose feet he could have touched without any effort, sat beside him, her eyes closed, her arms folded across her stomach. On the low table beside her stood a half empty cup of tea over which a skin had already formed. Norman began to hum but seeing his wife's closed eyes, stopped, listening instead to the sound of footsteps along the silent street.

Outside, the wind plucked the gulls and blew them like rags into the town, forcing them below the roofline where only their screams could be heard as they settled against the fire escapes and the tall, peeling backs of the empty holiday flats and guest houses.

At the appearance of the first rabbit, white and kicking, the children cheered. As the second and third were pulled into view they began to applaud. Some of them shouted, and the boiled sweets they were sucking fell out of their mouths on to the floor. The vicar's wife looked down as one bounced between her legs and came to rest against the front of the stage. She looked embarrassed and began to fondle her heavy necklace, smoothing the tiny conch shells down her bosom where they hung over its precipitous edge, swaying and clinking as she breathed.

As the third white rabbit came out of the hat she too applauded, encouraging the smaller, less certain children to do the same. She looked across the line of knees and saw her husband smiling at the rabbits and at the woman in the tight, sequin-covered costume who was taking them from the magician.

On stage, Derek Priestley pushed his hand through the false bottom of the hat for a fourth time, and holding the table steady, searched for the last rabbit. But the animal eluded him, hopping from side to side of the cage, keeping its ears flat and avoiding the fist which crashed around it. The children grew restless. Derek saw them and returned their smiles with a clenched grin. Cocking his head to one side he pointed upwards. This was intended to suggest to them that they should wait in silence, expectantly, ready to cheer. But many of the younger children misinterpreted the sign and gazed up at the ornate ceiling expecting to see something descend.

With a final blow – which missed the crouching animal completely – Derek withdrew his hand, the pattern of wire mesh imprinted across his knuckles, threatening to bleed. Turning, he told his audience that three rabbits was all they could expect with one chant of the magic spell. Many of the younger children continued staring at the ceiling. A small voice booed, and the vicar's wife turned in her seat.

Behind her husband, Veronica Priestley held up two of the three cooperative rabbits by their pink ears. One of the animals kicked the air with its hind feet. The other tensed itself into a begging position and hung there miserably. She swung them around, striking dramatic poses. The artistry of her performance was lost on the audience, the animals and her husband.

Derek readjusted his sleeve, careful to keep hidden the handkerchiefs and telescopic bouquets still attached to his forearm. The applause began to fade and Veronica swung the rabbits even higher in an attempt to revive it. It was a well-known fact that children liked rabbits, and for this reason the animals were produced and displayed as often as possible. 'Doctor Caligari's Magic Sword Cabinet' and her in fishnets and a bikini were bigger attractions at the Working Men's Clubs – where they appeared as 'The Fabulous Mantinis' – but children's performances were steady work and reasonably well paid, especially during the winter season, where provincial pantomimes were not what they had once been.

From the corner of her eye, Veronica watched the stage manager standing in the wings. He was leaning against a brightly painted, coffin-shaped box, waiting to push it on stage when directed.

'Smile, dearest,' Derek hissed through his smiling teeth. 'Show the little bleeders what they've come to see.'

She held the rabbits even higher. Her breasts rose and pushed together over the top of her low-cut and tightly fitting tunic.

'That's right, you stupid cow, and a nice bit of something for the Dads.'

Veronica swore and turned away, exposing what her dark stockings were intended to disguise. Depositing the two unhappy animals in a wicker basket, she dragged it offstage to where the stage manager waited.

Malcolm Devlin stared at the woman's breasts, saw her look up at him, but did nothing to disguise his interest. Instead, he smiled at her, following her along the narrow corridor which led away from the stage.

'Very nice. Very nice,' he said, watching as her breasts were flattened against the side of the coffin-shaped box.

From the stage, Derek Priestley looked to where his wife and Devlin stood. Veronica turned to watch her husband as he began folding a newspaper, tapping a jug of coloured water with his wand. Beside her, the Magic Sword Cabinet rocked. She steadied it and read the name spelled out along its side in cheap adhesive letters, black on gold, the type people bought to spell out the names of their homes stuck on to slices of varnished wood.

'Very original that. Very original.' Devlin resumed his conversation and gaze. 'Rabbits out of a top hat. Whatever next!'

The corridor behind them led to a flight of wooden stairs and another, even narrower corridor, along which the dressing rooms were situated. As with most provincial theatres struggling through the winter in a seaside town, the Royal Spa presented a pantomime devoid of the star names and attractions which filled it with holidaymakers in the summer. Also in common with most theatres, the décor and amenities backstage were considerably less than even the fading crimson carpet, flock wallpaper and gold-painted fittings of the foyer might suggest.

Above where Veronica and Devlin stood, the light from a single skylight faded.

'Coming on to rain,' he said.

She nodded. Without the light, the corridor seemed suddenly colder, and she rubbed her legs. He watched her and turned to look up at the dark shadow crossing the opaque glass. Throughout most of October it had remained surprisingly warm, but there seemed little chance now that the good weather would continue.

The afternoon performance had been arranged by the theatre manager following enquiries concerning a booking of all the local church youth groups. In what he considered to be a move of genius he presented them with a magic show and not the actual pantomime, hoping – rightly, as it turned out – that the children would insist upon coming back to see the full show.

The original theatre had been built upon the site of a dribbling natural well, whose untested waters were swiftly and enterprisingly endowed with medicinal powers to match those of any other spa and ensure the town of a future, however uncertain, as a tourist attraction. Hastily built to capitalise on the fashion for holidays by the sea, the original theatre, Baths and Rest Rooms had been as swiftly undermined by the stream which fed them. Now, whatever might have remained of the waters was channelled unseen and unmissed into the sea.

In the corridor, Devlin looked up to watch the first of the rain fall noisily on to the skylight. He swore silently at the thought of his journey home and at the cold which made him shiver.

*

'. . . are still concerned for the safety of Tracey Morton, the fourteen-year-old schoolgirl, who went missing from her home at 17 Queensway Drive last Saturday, and who has not been seen since. Tracey left home at approximately seven in the evening to visit friends. It was several hours later that the alarm was raised. When last seen, Tracey was wearing a black, knee-length skirt, red leg-warmers and a blue anorak with a pink rabbit motif on the breast pocket. She is five feet three inches tall, of slim build, and with brown eyes and hair. The police are particularly anxious to trace . . .'

Norman Protheroe, himself a police sergeant, mouthed each of the predictable sentences, switching off the radio and continuing loudly to their equally predictable conclusion. After thirty-three years on the force, his familiarity with the jargon was a source of great personal satisfaction. He spoke to the wall, crouching on all fours, his knees and back aching. Behind him, Alice said: 'Poor little kiddy . . .'

Norman tutted and repeated her words, raising his voice to a tone of mock incredulity. It was the tone he used when people told him they didn't know the frame numbers of their stolen bicycles, or when they arrived to report people whose dogs had fouled the pavement. ' "Poor little kiddy! Poor little kiddy?" '

Alice peered over the ornate rims of her knitting glasses and told him there was no need to adopt that tone with her. Norman apologised.

'I was only thinking of the poor girl's mother: she must be worried half out of her mind.'

'Run off most like,' he said, straightening the knot of navy-blue tie and smoothing its length over his pale blue shirt, still on all fours, watching his reflection in the glass-fronted cabinet.

Alice studied his back and the girdle of fat which squeezed above his belt. Nodding again, she dislodged her glasses and returned them to their case.

'*Great Rivers of the World*,' he said. 'Have you seen it?'

Anyone else might have made a joke, but not Alice. What time did she have for rivers? 'To the left of *Unknown Tibet*.'

Norman pulled out the heavy, colourful book. 'Irriwady, Nile, Mississippi . . .' he began. *Unknown Tibet* slid from the cabinet unassisted and fell open at a two-page spread entitled 'Majestic Splendour' whose black, blue and white composition of ice and sky fared badly against his wife's colourful carpet with

13

its spiralling leaf design of orange, brown and yellow. She watched the pages as they slapped over, one at a time, hypnotically almost, settling gently at 'Majestic Splendour', subtitled 'Everest in Spring', but which, without her glasses, she could not read.

Norman was saying something about discharges and about the Post Office Tower going over Niagara Falls six times every minute.

'It's been proved,' he said, closing the book on his hand and changing the subject, 'that in captivity, squids commit suicide by eating their own tentacles and—'

'Norman! The things—'

'Jack Cousteau, 1968.'

'*Great Rivers?*'

'*The Sea Around Us.* Chapter three.'

For her husband's sake, Alice tried occasionally to appear interested, but she cared little for the unexplored depths or the wonders of the natural world. And besides, at fifty-five she considered this resurgence of interest on Norman's part as something similar to a second childhood, something to be tolerated though not actively encouraged.

She said, 'Oh,' and picking up the *TV Times*, she read about Liberace's diamond bath taps, repeating aloud various phrases for him to hear. 'Piano-shaped sponges . . . solid gold plug . . .' But Norman, eyes closed, intoning length, volume and date of discovery of the Nile, was not listening.

Norman was captain of the local Inter-County Constabulary Quiz team, in which Great Rivers and Unknown Lands featured prominently. Fully apprised of the Mighty Nile, he turned to the photograph of a transparent fish. Not once in six years as captain had it occurred to Norman that an Unknown Land about which someone could compile a large and colourful book cannot have been as unknown as all that. But knowledge was knowledge, and he peered closely at the insides of the transparent fish, at its belly full of sucked worms and at the short arrow pointing to its beating heart.

'Mink-upholstered Rolls-Royce,' Alice said, but still he wasn't listening. She sat back in her chair, closed her eyes and stroked her arms.

'. . . own weight in food every two hours. And that's without any eyes.' He turned to show her the blue and yellow outline of the fish. But Alice did not see them. He looked from the face of his wife to that of Liberace on the cover of the magazine. 'No eyes,' he repeated, and turned away.

Tracey Morton, the missing girl about whom there was currently so much concern was, in fact, already dead. She had been assaulted, killed, and partially buried less than twenty minutes after leaving her home, and a little under four hours before the alarm was raised. The distance between where she had been assaulted and killed and where her body had been hastily buried was less than twelve yards. It was, in fact, less than half that distance from the boundary of Norman's own allotment – a coincidence which was to cause him considerable embarrassment when discovered.

Tracey had struggled, she had screamed, and she had shouted, but this had done her little good, and had in all likelihood contributed to her death. She had been beaten and then strangled with her own red leg-warmer. With the exception of the second leg-warmer, she was naked from the waist down when found. It was her foot, protruding from beneath the pile of waste and soil under which her body had been hidden, which led to her eventual discovery, and from which the enquiry into her death was put into motion, hopelessly late and with little conviction that the murder would ever be solved. The leg-warmer with which she had been strangled – strands of which were found in her mouth and hair – was never recovered. Her shoes and handbag had been buried with the body.

Exchanging *Great Rivers* for a book on the Pacific Ocean, in which over four thousand islands were listed by name, Norman marvelled at the bone-white horseshoes of brittle coral reefs. 'Marvelled' is perhaps too strong a word, but this is what he was invited to do by the publishers, confident of his Complete Satisfaction. The colour of the book, unlike the turgid and steaming browns of the Dark Continent, was largely blue – pale blue, dark blue, sky blue and white where the sea made contact with the fringes of the land.

He half turned to show Alice. But Alice was still asleep and perhaps dreaming of driving with Liberace in his sable-lined Mercedes.

It was half past ten, windy and raining. Soon he would have to wake her, a task which always caused him an inexplicable feeling of guilt. And, once awake, she would complain at not having been woken sooner. She would look at the clock, get up and walk into the kitchen, from which the sound of a boiling kettle and the rattle of crockery would soon issue as she prepared a late supper for their guests.

Norman returned his books to the cabinet. Then he sat in his chair, interlocked his fingers, and awaited the return of Derek and Veronica Priestley, of blonde and black-haired Rita, and of Mighty Morgan, 'Midget Man of Muscle'.

Mighty Morgan, Midget Man of Muscle, tore the ever-increasing pile of cardboard boxes into flat sheets and fed them into the baling machine which compressed them and tied them with wire into compact bundles. In addition to breaking the boxes flat, he had also to feed the machine with its coils of greased wire and to manoeuvre the solid bales into a small, litter-strewn yard behind the supermarket.

Mighty Morgan swore. He cursed the job, the money, the pantomime, the weather, the town, and the manager of the store who treated him like a child. He cursed Alice and Norman Protheroe; he cursed their home and then the theatre at which he appeared nightly, strutting onstage to frighten the children and pantomime horse. (Booo! Behind You!! Look Out!!! The words still echoed in that small room and he cursed the screamers and their parents for bringing them.)

In the baling machine a full bottle of tomato sauce burst with a loud crack, seeping from between the slices of card. In the warehouse he heard the voices of the till girls, and shelf fillers and stock managers. He heard the suppressed laughter and then the running footsteps of those responsible for the bottle.

Morgan leapt once into the air and swore. The short, awkward leap was an automatic response, one learned in the circus where he had performed and been exhibited since his birth, and where such gestures were encouraged. The circus had named him and he had read his name on the colourful posters with their borders of lions and tigers with pride and then despair. To keep secret his body-building rise from midget to Man of Muscle, he had hung net curtains at the windows of his caravan. A year from beginning to end had been his proud boast – at which an acrobat had remarked that it should only have taken him six months because he was only half a man. A month later, the acrobat had broken a leg, knocked down by a florist's van. Morgan had considered this revenge enough. A year later the lion died and the small circus folded. He remembered the animal's body, like a large, badly stuffed toy, patchy and worn on the surface.

The road from the circus to novelty appearances at panto-mimes had been a short and painful one.

The sauce began to drip and seeing it Morgan growled. This, too, was a circus response. The dead lion had been collected by two men with a lorry, its limbs flopping over its bloated belly and its head swinging loosely as they attached chains and dragged it away.

'Mind you, snakes were always one of the biggest attractions in my line of work. Work with snakes and you'd always be sure of bookings. There was a girl did round Hartlepool – Irma something-or-other – she had snakes. Two. Big black and yellow things they were. Thick as – no, stop it, don't make me laugh – thick as your leg.'

The man looked from his crotch to his leg, blew out a mouthful of smoke and laughed.

'I thought for a minute you were going to say something else.' He laughed again, killing the joke with a drink which dripped from the bottom of his glass. Rita hit him playfully and laughed with him. He touched her empty glass with his own. She smiled, straightened her short coat and crossed her legs, touching his foot with the point of her shoe. As she moved, the stool upon which she sat rocked, and she held the bar for support. It was evident to everyone but herself that she was drunk. The man put out his hand as though to steady her and then withdrew without touching her. He tapped her glass again and shouted over his shoulder, knocking the two glasses on the polished wood.

'Still do a bit, do you? Still . . .'

'No, nothing much in that line,' she lied, tilting her head backwards and blowing a feather of smoke towards the ceiling. 'Not got the figure for it, see. Not any more.' Now she was fishing for his denial, a drunken compliment. But the man had turned away and was paying for their drinks. He had missed a chance. When he turned back to face her, she returned to the topic of the snakes.

'Anacondas,' she said, uncertain, but knowing it was the name

17

of a snake. The man slid her glass towards her and nodded.

'Anacondas, eh,' he said, fingering her jacket and muttering something she couldn't hear. Now he sounded offended. A line of cream froth hung across his lip.

'Yes, they were always a big pull. No trouble getting into the clubs with a snake. Novelty, see. Something a bit . . .' She looked down into the remains of ice and lemon in her glass, spinning it and remembering.

The man had turned away again and was laughing with two others. She smiled at them. He whispered something and they looked back to where she sat. She tried not to hear what they were saying.

'Get a good crowd in here on a Sunday dinnertime,' he said, turning back to her and watching her empty glass, measuring it against his own progress and deciding she would have to wait.

From an adjoining room came the sound of an organ and then someone singing. She saw a man with an open shirt, frilled at the front. He was singing with his eyes closed, as though imagining himself elsewhere. 'The Green, Green Grass of Home.' Even the songs were the same.

Above the bar hung a naked woman whose charms became increasingly apparent with every packet of peanuts bought. Rita looked up and smiled, half raising her glass in an empty gesture which she did not understand.

'Not known any strippers before,' the man said, buoyed now by the drink and the half circle of men to whom his conquest was becoming enviably clear as they neared closing time and their own wives and children and homes. Five years ago the words would have encouraged her, but now she said nothing. Through the picture window, she could see the sea but she was not impressed by it. Above the window hung straw-coated bottles, plastic flowers and notices advertising basket meals which no one ordered. A net hung with plastic crabs and lobsters stretched the full length of the view.

Outside, the sea rose to its drumming, crashing unnoticed against the chalk cliffs which stretched away to the north of the town. Beside the harbour, over which the window looked, a lifeboat sat poised at the head of its concrete ramp. A man walked around it, banging his fists against the hull.

Another tap of her glass, another drink, and she was beyond

caring, resigned to what the man was buying and her own unspoken part of the bargain.

'Born and bred here myself,' he boasted. 'Man and boy.'

'Leeds,' she said, lying again, and then thinking of her two children and wondering how they might look, how they had grown up and what their names might be.

'You'll have seen a fair bit yourself, then,' he said. She nodded, shook the thoughts from her head and decided to talk to him. He asked her what she was doing in the town and she told him. She told him about the pantomime, about her part in it, and where she was staying. He told her he knew the road and made his knowledge sound impressive.

Her part in the dance troupe had been acquired for her by a man who had once acted as her agent. She was there because he had guaranteed six dancers and upon the date agreed could find only five. Initially, she had been flattered by her inclusion in the troupe. It was only as she heard the audience's laughter on the opening night that she realised what a ridiculous spectacle they made. Still, it was regular work for a minimum of six weeks, and the agent had offered to try and find her something locally in her usual line. So far there had been nothing.

'Not much I don't get to know about,' the man said. She smiled at him and said he must be fairly well known. This pleased him and he smiled back.

'Oh, ask anybody. They all know me.' And he told her his name but she forgot it and it didn't matter.

'Ken Dodd,' he said. 'We had Ken Dodd this summer. Always get somebody big for the summer.'

Behind the bar a bell was rung and the landlord shouted. Men queued and jostled, and on the floor a glass shattered. 'Only one pair of hands,' the barmaid said.

Across the ceiling, fluorescent lights stammered into life. The men shouted their goodbyes and the room emptied. In five hours they would be back.

Still unnoticed and unremarked, the sea punched at the cliffs, undercutting them and scouring out great caves the size of churches.

At 6.50 Tracey left her home at 17 Queensway Drive. By 7.05 she was probably already dead. Her murderer might have approached her, asked her the time or for directions, or might possibly have said something more overtly sinister before grabbing hold of her, his hand over her mouth, and dragging her into the shadow of an empty building which bordered the allotments. Tracey probably screamed. Girls of that age are very good screamers, and given the chance she would have attracted attention to her plight and perhaps have frightened off her attacker. Unfortunately, those nearest the scene of this attack and subsequent murder were not in an ideal position to either hear or do anything about whatever might have been happening.

The Mansley Terrace Darby and Joan Club, a wooden hut which was shared with the Methodists on Fridays and with the Christian Scientists when required, stood only forty yards beyond the allotments on the opposite side of Queensway Drive. On the night in question, starting at six-thirty, those assembled at the club were enjoying the first event of their long Christmas programme – in this instance a retired military man showing a slide show and giving a talk on his days as a District Commissioner in West Africa. The dark curtains had been drawn, and all eyes and functioning ears had been on the speaker as he pointed with a slender stick to the naked breasts of grinning pigmy women. 'Pigmies, ladies and gentlemen, BaMbuti pigmies.' 'Oh, ooh, ah. Fancy that!' Applause, uncertain, but swelling. Next slide: more small brown men, this time with an antelope and even broader smiles than their wives and daughters. 'Roast it whole and eat it at a single sitting.' (A discussion on the cost of meat.) 'Grand little chaps.' More naked breasts, ritually scarred with bubbles of hot ash forced beneath the skin. Arms pressed self-consciously to their sides. (Jokes from old and widowed Arthur Smedley about swinging tits.) Next slide. Unwieldy blowpipes accurate up to forty yards to kill a parrot. (Arthur Smedley: 'What sort of parrot?' If the truth were told, Arthur Smedley had become something of an embarrassment with his lewd manners and foul language.)

So the curtains were drawn and the lights dimmed as Tracey was assaulted and strangled only forty yards away. (The same distance as the effective range of the BaMbuti blowpipe – a coincidence on which no one afterwards thought to remark.)

Tracey might have screamed, but those collected at the Darby and Joan club were too involved with the West African rain forest to hear. (Weeks later, and as a direct result of the slide show, the police notebooks were found to reveal a variety of strange and remarkable facts concerning the rain forest and the BaMbuti tribe and their customs – little of which was to be of any real help in the search for Tracey's killer, but none of which was ultimately to be wasted on Norman Protheroe.)

'According to this, if one snail eats another snail then it absorbs the memory of the snail it eats.'

Alice Protheroe crossed the kitchen. In one hand she held a roll of silver foil, and in the other a thawing chicken. A line of watery drops of blood traced her path across the white and yellow tiles. She sang along with the radio and counted out potatoes from a sack, estimating the number required to feed six people. After twenty-four years as a seaside landlady, little guesswork was involved. She stopped. Norman had shouted something about snails.

'Where?' she shouted back, and looked instinctively down for the tell-tale silver lines which sometimes appeared during the winter.

'South America, I suppose.'

'Oh.' And still not really understanding, she dropped the chicken on to her Formica working surface, where she carved it mentally into six and thought about stock for a casserole.

In the living room, Norman traced the lines about the snails and shook his head. He did not stop to consider why one snail should wish to absorb the memory of another, or what, when absorbed, that second memory added to the first. There was not, after all, a great deal that can have been very exciting about a snail's memory. And so he turned back to the picture of a tapir and its young and remembered the occasion when, as quiz captain, he had correctly identified and described a collared peccary.

'Battenburg or trifle?' Alice held the puddings, one in each hand, as if one or the other should be chosen according to their weight. Norman said, 'Battenburg,' and she returned to the kitchen.

' "Foul play is not suspected," ' Norman read. 'Foul Play.' The words were his favourites. Foul Play is not suspected. Foul Play is suspected. They said everything and nothing. Even taken separately the words remained ambiguous, capable of any interpretation. The words put people on their guard. Men and women, mothers and fathers who had not even dreamt that anything untoward had happened were suddenly shocked, making up their own minds and warning their own daughters. 'Nothing Untoward' might have meant the same, but that was too . . . too imprecise.

Norman read the article twice, absorbing the details of appearance, of dress, of where she had come from and where she was going. There were details about everything except what really mattered. 'Known Facts.' Another favourite. The report made reference to a similar disappearance seven years ago when a thirteen-year-old girl had gone missing and had never been traced. She, too, had . . . had . . . Had what? Disappeared? Everyone pointed to these coincidences, but seldom was anything achieved by it. And, as Norman knew, these past crimes were only dug out as fillers. 'Most crime is boring, day to day routine.' That was the Chief Superintendent's weekly reminder. He meant, of course, crime detection, but no one – least of all Norman – was going to point out his mistake.

In the kitchen Alice peeled potatoes and began to wonder if she hadn't made a mistake in taking in Mighty Morgan. No one could accuse her of prejudice (she would say), but all the same . . . There was something about him which made her uneasy. The others were regulars, back most winters, but in future she would think twice about ex-circus people, and midgets in particular. Veronica and Derek Priestley were a different kettle of fish altogether, perfect guests, her in her dresses and him with his bow tie. Dressing for all his meals, and so polite. In their room she ran her hand over Veronica's costumes and stroked the silk of his top hat, dropping it in alarm when the false bottom clapped suddenly open. She had replaced it, still open, on their crowded dressing table and lived with her guilty secret all day. That evening, waiting till Derek was alone, she told him what had happened. And what a gentleman. 'Not to trouble yourself, dear Mrs Protheroe.' He had pulled a bouquet of paper flowers from his sleeve with a flourish and presented them to her, explaining how the flourish was designed to open them out. What he did not point out was that this particular bunch was getting a little frayed around the edges.

'Raining!' Norman shouted. She shouted back that he had nearly given her a heart attack. The molten lard with which she basted the chicken splashed on to her arm. She left the kitchen to stand beside him.

'We'll have to get some more pellets to put down,' she said.
'Pellets?'
'For the slugs.'
'Oh.'
She sat on the sofa opposite him.
'It's still raining,' he repeated after a minute's silence.
Alice heard him, watched him, shook her head, and considered all her Lost and Wasted Opportunities. That was what she called them, but she was never any more specific about what she meant or what they might have been.

Veronica peered through the side curtain at the rows of screaming children. On stage, Morgan dodged between her husband and a screen, running out when Derek's back was turned. She watched them and saw the complete lack of emotion on the faces of both men. At one point Morgan had slipped and there had been a lull in the shouting. Her husband had had to compensate for the delay – which he did as always by staring up at the ornate ceiling, closing his eyes and swearing under his breath.

Seeing the men made Veronica consider her own position. She often tried looking ahead, but the thought of where she might still be in the years to come, of what she might still be doing, depressed her. Equally, looking back offered her little hope of any real improvement: school, seven years as a hairdresser and then the lure of Derek and showbusiness, both of which had rapidly faded in their appeal. She could not decide whether she hated Derek because of what they had to do together or whether she hated what they did simply because she hated him so much. Perhaps life would have been more bearable with someone else as a partner? She often thought of these things, especially during their winter engagements, which were shorter, less well paid and less certain.

The children resumed their screaming as Morgan dashed out like a cornered animal. Her husband looked to the wings. To avoid him Veronica resumed the search of her tights, testing both legs for holes and dabbing nail varnish beneath one knee. Lifting her leg, she blew on the spot, flinching at the smell and holding the bottle at arm's length. Along the corridor, Devlin manoeuvred a chest towards the stage, making no attempt to deaden the noise as he dragged it over the wooden floor. She watched him but said nothing. What did she care? He stopped beside her, nodding at her outstretched legs which blocked the narrow passage.

'Shift the fuckin' things.' He spoke without removing his cigarette.

'Always the gentleman.' And she lifted her legs higher, in a showgirl pose, smiling coyly.

'You really fuckin' fancy yourself, don't you?' he said, unable to either move or take his eyes from the flesh of her thighs. He rubbed the fingers of one hand over his palm, as though in some way testing his own response to the woman's provocation.

'Third fuckin' rate performers, you are. Third rate.'

'And what are you? A caretaker,' she replied, maintaining her provocative pose and fluttering her eyelashes. 'A caretaker. A nobody. N.O.B.O.D.Y.'

Beside her were piled the open-sided wicker baskets in which the rabbits were huddled, their act finished. The animals were kept at the theatre overnight and it was Devlin's responsibility to care for them. Consequently, it was upon the rabbits, two to each basket, that he exacted his revenge. Sometimes he starved them, sometimes he shook the baskets, and once he had thrown them to the floor and kicked them.

'Watch what the fu—' and he began coughing.

The children were silent, watching Derek as he manipulated the wires of a rubber ball which rose, supposedly unaided, beneath a blue silk handkerchief. Behind his screen, Morgan squatted, waiting discontentedly until his next appearance in a few minutes' time. After that he would dash from the stage accompanied by the booing of the children. Veronica would step out to take his place and the booing would turn to cheers.

Devlin's coughing subsided and he sat beside her on the baskets of rabbits whose lids sagged dangerously. He settled himself against her, his leg touching hers for a moment before she became aware of it and moved away. He looked at the crescents of red on her thighs where the costume bit into her flesh.

'Nasty, that,' he said. 'You want to lose a bit of weight.'

She looked down and turned away. She wanted to rub where the elastic bit, but did not. With practised slowness Devlin looked up her legs, crotch and stomach to where her breasts, pushed above the tasselled V of her neckline, rose and fell as she breathed. He continued to rub his fingers across his palm, pausing only to screw his cigarette into the floor with his foot. Immediately he lit another, offering one to Veronica. She accepted. He touched her hand, steadying it as he held out his lighter. She took a deep breath, holding her head back to blow smoke upwards. He watched her neck and saw the loose skin of her chin stretch and disappear.

The sound of running feet made them both turn and they watched as six small girls dressed as daisies in green and white ran along the narrow space and queued, in order of height, waiting to rush on to the stage and work through their dance routine. They would be accompanied by six small boys dressed as bees in black and yellow stripes who would buzz among them, much to the delight of their parents.

Devlin pushed the tallest and oldest girl, telling her to watch where she was going. Veronica blew smoke over the children and they rubbed their eyes. The youngest looked about to cry. All six shivered and rubbed their bare arms and legs.

'Got any kids yourself, have you?' The cigarette in Devlin's mouth rose and fell. The children flinched. Veronica shook her head. 'No? Best off without. Bloody nuisances if you ask me.' He turned to watch the girls, smiling at them and causing them to bunch even more closely together.

In the opposite wing, Veronica saw Roland Trotter, the theatre manager. He stood facing her with a cigar between his lips. He smiled at her, nodded towards the audience and her husband, and clapped silently, his hands never meeting. Then he saw Devlin sitting beside her and his smile faltered.

The six daisies ran on to the stage and began their flimsy dance. From behind Roland Trotter came the bees.

Veronica watched and smiled involuntarily. Morgan ran to where she and Devlin stood, carrying his screen like a shield. Derek, drawing one last rise in the applause, stood at the edge of the stage and continued to bow, waving his gloved hands in elaborate curling gestures.

Roland Trotter watched the dance of the bees. Whilst he never underestimated the appeal of children, he too had little time for them and, with a dismissive gesture, he walked away. His own dislike was born of the fact that he had three children of his own and a wife who devoted all of her time and most of his money towards providing them with the things he himself had never had, and which he resented them having. Consequently, his offspring drifted around his luxury bungalow like a school of pampered and overweight whales, his wife at their head. Their fatness didn't bother him, and in some ways he preferred it to the slight stature of the daisies and bees weaving in and out before him. A fat child, he considered, was better able to withstand a blow than a thin one.

The bungalow, built to his own ostentatious design, had become a playground within which their every whim was indulged. Built on the better side of town, it had Georgian windows and Grecian pillars fronting the doorway. From inside, looking out over the sea, Roland Trotter would sit and consider his position. On the wall beside his swivelling chair hung a ship's wheel, an accompanying brass plaque proving its authenticity (he had insisted on the plaque and never failed to point it out).

The bungalow sat between the town and Danes Head, the chalk peninsula on which the lighthouse stood (and which, at night, Roland would draw back the curtains to reveal). Beyond the bungalow, and expensively screened with red and yellow evergreens, stood the first of the caravan camps. Beyond these, between the village and the lighthouse, stood the line of weatherboard chalets in which Devlin lived with his mother.

Roland Trotter left the dancing children and walked back to his office. He paused to listen to a burst of applause, and he too began to clap as the daisies, still pursued by the bees, raced past him along the narrow corridor.

2

Following an hour of drunken deliberation, a bruised rib and a black eye, Vincent had been committed to court and found guilty of aggravated assault upon Maureen, his wife. It was, he insisted, he who had been the aggrieved party, but following the advice of his legal aid solicitor he had said nothing and had sailed through his brief trial under the shaky flag of mitigating circumstances.

Sentenced to one year, he served nine months in an open prison near Nottingham.

When he was sober, he and Maureen were evenly matched, and when he was sober he sought to avoid rather than confront her. On the occasion leading to his trial and eventual imprisonment he had afforded her the upper hand by virtue of his drunkenness. She, as a result, had taken advantage of him and drawn blood. He had collapsed, more in shock than as a result of the wound. Even then it would have gone no further had a neighbour not intervened and called for the police who, seeing blood and a spilled cutlery drawer, had radioed for an ambulance – much to the delight of the four small children lining the staircase. The neighbour, it transpired, had been waiting for just such an opportunity to gain her revenge following the escape of Vincent's chickens into the garden where her husband grew – had grown – prize chrysanthemums.

Even at her husband's brief and predictable hearing, Maureen had warmed to the Mitigating Circumstances and had spoken – or, rather, shouted out of turn – on his behalf. 'A little tiff,' she had called it, smiling at the lady magistrate before making the mistake of asking her if she and *her* husband didn't have them. Vincent smiled and winked at his wife before turning to nod at the austere-looking woman above him. This, in effect, sealed his fate. Behind him, his solicitor sighed.

Now Vincent walked the streets, constantly returning to look out over the sea. He was in the town because of his sister, Alice.

Vincent's real names were Arthur Peter, but these he considered too ordinary. The name tattooed across the knuckles of his left hand was Elvis. Elvis is love, he would explain when drunk, lashing out, the word in full – albeit momentary – display, at anyone who disagreed.

He stood in shop doorways, looking over the grey sea, his collar ineffectually turned against the occasional needles of rain. He scanned the deserted streets in the hope of seeing Alice, of catching her alone and explaining his plight before Norman learned of his presence. It was because of Norman that he did not go directly to the house – because he was a policeman, and because he, Vincent, had been a criminal, largely petty and undetected, for most of his life. In the doorways he smoked his cigarettes and searched the faces of the passing shoppers.

One consolation during Vincent's time in prison had been the discovery of twenty-three other Elvis fans, with whom he subsequently formed (and became chairman of) a Prisoners' Elvis Appreciation Society, which, in the absence of a record player, devoted most of its time to comparing each others' tattoos and photographs cut from magazines. All this, unfortunately, came to an end with the stabbing of Boy Elvis, 21, homosexual car thief of Nuneaton. The fact that the society had harboured a homosexual – and all this implied about The King – caused considerably more consternation amongst the members than the stabbing itself.

Vincent's memories of the Appreciation Society were happy ones, and with them he cut out the rain and the wind and the cold. But they could sustain him for only so long. From the Lifeboat Snack Bar came the sweet smell of tea. He went inside, startled momentarily by the bell which sprang to life and caused everyone to turn and watch him enter. At the table with his tea, he thought about Alice and debated his chances of being able to stay with her until he either found a job or returned to Maureen. Steam ran down the café window, washing the whitewashed menu into an indecipherable pattern of plain food and cheap prices.

Alice was Vincent's older sister by almost fifteen years. Until she left home they had been very close and before his own marriage, thirteen years ago, he had visited her at least once a year. Then Norman had put his foot down. They were being imposed upon, he insisted, and added, with characteristic bias, that Vincent had never made anything of his life and would come to no good. It was because of the fondly remembered holidays and Vincent's unexpressed but sincere feelings for his sister that he had come to the town upon his release from prison. For two hours he sat with two cups of tea, watching the sea, the rain, the steam and the disappearing price list.

The chances were, he reasoned, that Norman would be on duty and, it being out of season, Alice would be at home, alone. He did not know then, of course, about Derek and Veronica, about Rita or Mighty Morgan. Equally, he did not appreciate the significance of the missing girl and the police's increased vigilance for strange faces and all this implied concerning his own arrival. Whereas in summer the population of the town quadrupled, in winter a solitary stranger stood out.

An hour later, Vincent left the café and was forced by the returning rain into the empty waiting room of the bus station. There, with his hands pressed to a lukewarm radiator, he realised that he was not yet ready for Norman. Tomorrow, perhaps, the winter sun would be shining and everything would be easier. In the waiting room he read a poster for the pantomime, vaguely remembering a happy childhood visit.

A bus arrived and a queue of old people moved towards it. Its destination was Danes Head and then the Lighthouse. To arrive there it passed through Danes Head village and along the roads which skirted the empty caravan sites. He boarded the bus and settled against a wet window, watching the rows of dull lights as they faded behind him.

Alice, oblivious of her brother's proximity, pressed the button and waited for the traffic to pass. She read the advertisements pasted along the side of the bus upon which Vincent now sat. A young woman arrived beside her pushing a pram, a box-like structure of polythene in which a child was being nurtured like a rare orchid. Alice looked for a face but saw only the reflection of her own and those of the shop lights in the shallow pool of water which had collected above the child's head. 'Nasty weather,' the woman said, and banged her heels against the kerb, impatient at the lights and passing traffic.

Occasionally, Alice still thought of her brother, and during the first week of his imprisonment she had visited him. Norman, to his credit, had said very little about Vincent at the time. On occasions though he still gave her brief lectures on what the Law was and why it needed to be upheld. It was partly because of her husband's profession and way of life, Alice realised, that her own feelings of shame at her brother's imprisonment had been so great. Being a policeman entailed certain responsibilities and commitments which were not to be dismissed lightly. Accordingly, Norman lived by the Law and Alice lived in fear of it.

Her shopping completed, Alice settled into a corner seat at the Cosy Kettle, where her requests for tea never varied and where she was never tempted by the display of dry pastries. The waitresses all knew her but, as is the way with seaside waitresses, none of them spoke to her as they took her order, writing it in their pads and tearing out carbon copies which they slapped down like summonses.

Sometimes, Alice would meet other landladies and they would complain together at their off-season problems, at their costly renovations, their hopes for the coming summer and whatever else passed for gossip to sustain them through the winter months.

But today there was no one, and as she sat alone, pouring cups of tea from the aluminium pot, she felt uneasy. She could not explain why, but she felt distinctly unsettled, as though something was going to happen or was already happening which had some bearing upon her life and the routine by which she lived. She had felt like this for several days, searching the conversations and actions of her guests for some clue to the cause of her unease.

For the past week she had woken in the middle of the night looking for the outline of grey light through the curtain to gain some indication of the time. She had been oppressively anxious, as though waking from a violent and disturbing dream. And, once awake, she had begun to worry about things she would previously have laughed at. Everybody, she knew, had their hopes and dreams, and nobody was too surprised when they came to nothing. But there was something else – an emptiness, an inexplicable frustration which worried her. Winters depressed her. The town died, and part of her along with it. In summer there were tens of thousands of holidaymakers pulsing through the streets, spending money and enjoying themselves, and the town responded. But now, in winter, it lay in a kind of suspended animation with only the uncertain prospect of a good season ahead to keep it alive.

Alice poured her third cup and watched her distorted features looking back from the polished brass kettle hanging beside her.

She glanced at it as she drank, seeing someone else, turning away to avoid being seen. Other reflections moved around her. She knew they were hers, fragmented and misshapen, and to avoid seeing them she sat with her hands held to the sides of her face.

The Cosy Kettle was a popular café, and though its proprietress thought it more up-market than the majority of her clientele, it received sufficient custom to enable it to remain open during the winter months. What Alice did not know was that the waitress who had served her, the forty-year-old woman whose hair fell over one eye in an untidy spiral, was the mother of the missing girl. Alice saw only the hair, the dark eyes and flushed face. No helper of hers would be allowed to handle food looking like that. She watched the woman as she tugged at the stray hairs, pushing them behind her ear.

The girl, her daughter, had been missing for over a week and the woman had been advised to carry on as closely as possible to normal. Each day her daughter was missing, the policewoman had assured her, the better were the chances of her only having run off. She was going to add that as a rule most bodies turn up reasonably quickly, often between one and ten days after the act whereby they become bodies (and consequently eligible for the police to use the convenient euphemisms which distinguish them very clearly from the people – or schoolgirls – they once were). In the case of Tracey Morton, of course, the one to ten day rule was not to apply. The policewoman did not mention that there was a threshold beyond which the chances of the girl being found well and alive began to diminish. By a strange coincidence, that threshold – calculated on individual circumstances, and thus allowing for hope where none should reasonably exist – was eight weeks, and occurred, in this instance, on Christmas Day.

But Alice knew none of this as she watched the woman and as she concentrated on draining the last of the tea from her small pot. This, she considered, was reasonable value for money when heating and lighting were taken into consideration.

After half an hour Alice left the café. It was still raining and the streets still shone, but in that half hour the night had drawn in, and now, at three-thirty, it was already dark. She walked beneath shop canopies, close to open crates of fruit and vegetables, of satsumas and walnuts selling early for Christmas. She passed the deserted cinema and the warm doorways out of which men, warmth, noise, and the mixed smells of drink and tobacco now spilled. She watched the men and envied them their ability to be loud and carefree at such a time.

Crossing the road, she walked briefly along the Promenade before returning home. Passing where the harbour steps ran down to the waterless basin of mud, she paused to watch a solitary figure walking alone along the harbour wall.

Malcolm Devlin stood with his face to the sea and with one foot resting on the silver railings which separated him from the dirty waves curling up the concave wall beneath him, its skirt of green weed marking the high water line yet to be reached. He watched the gulls, being blown and buffeted by the wind, and the broken sea driving in white lines against the base of the cliffs.

Throwing down his cigarette, he watched it explode in a scatter of sparks against the stone at his feet. Rubbing a gloved hand over his face, he turned from the water and walked slowly back to the theatre.

'How's it going then, love?' Derek Priestley handed the plate of sliced and buttered bread over the crowded table to Rita. Beside him, his wife stuck her fork into the meat on her plate, drawing its juice and pulling a face at the result.

'Oh, all right.' Rita smiled and thanked him for the bread.

In the doorway stood Alice. She looked along the table at each of her guests, seeing how much meat, how many potatoes and vegetables had been eaten. Norman stood behind her, a plate in his hand, impatient to begin his own meal. Usually he preferred to eat separately, but tonight his shift had coincided with their gathering.

'Still doing the stripping on the side?' Veronica asked loudly, looking at Rita and smiling for the benefit of her husband.

At the end of the table, raised on his seat of cushions, sat Morgan. He began to hum the stripper's tune, tapping his fork against the side of his plate, gently at first and then louder. Alice turned to her husband with a puzzled look, and Derek told Morgan to stop the racket and let them eat their meal in a civilised manner. Having said this, he turned and shared a smile with Alice, who seldom addressed Morgan directly.

From Derek, Alice looked to Veronica, and then across to Rita. The two women still stared at each other and the juices continued to rise in drops from Veronica's meat. Later, Derek would say something to his wife about her unkind remark to Rita, but at the table he had to keep up appearances and so remained silent. Rita watched him and smiled. She realised what was happening between him and Veronica. Morgan continued to hum quietly.

'Yes, well, if we can all . . .' Norman walked to the empty seat. 'Shall we all . . .?' It was his way of announcing his presence and letting them know that there were levels of behaviour and conduct which he considered he had the right to expect from them whilst they were in his home. Sitting between Veronica and the end of the table, he felt a man apart. Opposite him, Morgan ate with his mouth open and with a line of gravy down one side of his chin.

'Alice was saying as how you have rabbits, Mr Priestley,' Norman said. He might have said a thousand things, but it served to break the silence.

'Yes. Rabbits and doves. Doves, too. Please, call me Derek.' Both men leaned back in their seats to face each other. Between them, Veronica bent forward to her plate.

'Rabbits and doves. Mmm nice.' Then, suddenly: 'Myxomatosis. Wiped out Australia's rabbits just like that!' He banged his knife against the table to emphasise his words.

'Yes, I er . . . myxo . . . Yes, I'd heard it er . . .' Veronica sat back, coming between the two men and smiling at her husband as he tried unsuccessfully to hide his ignorance.

Norman leaned forward but Derek stayed where he was, having no wish to continue a discussion on a subject about which he knew nothing.

'Yes, Derek knows all about rabbits, don't you dear?' Veronica pulled out her fork. 'Not much you can tell Derek about rabbits, is there?' She drew her lips into a stage smile and turned from Norman to her husband, chewing slowly.

'No, I . . . er, rabbits and doves. Four rabbits, six birds.'

'Myxo – what's that, then?' Morgan pointed his knife.

'Go on, Derek, tell the Mighty Midget what it is.' She stopped chewing.

'Well, it's a . . . Well, er . . . Perhaps Mr Protheroe might like to explain. I only use English rabbits and of course I'm more concerned with the pulling-out-of-hats side of things.' He laughed. Norman laughed with him and Veronica straightened her smile.

'Myx-o-ma-to-sis.' Norman stressed each syllable and began to describe the physical effects of the disease. Rita tried to look interested and Veronica stopped eating.

The description was cut short by Alice who said 'Norman! People are eating!'

'Sorry, dear, but I was only . . . Mister, er, Morgan wanted to know about . . .'

'Well, I'm sure he didn't expect – didn't want to hear about things like that.'

Morgan smiled at them both, pleased at being the cause of their brief conflict. Both misinterpreted his smile in their favour and smiled back. Alice turned back into the kitchen and Norman whispered that he had a photograph. Perhaps they could have a look at it afterwards. Morgan nodded and dropped half a slice of bread on to his plate.

For a full minute there was silence, broken only by Derek saying, 'Lovely tea, Alice.' Everybody turned. Derek pointed to his empty plate and felt immediately self-conscious. Norman wondered when the change from 'Mrs Protheroe' to 'Alice' had occurred.

'Thank you, Derek. It's nice to know you're appreciated.'

Norman looked from his wife to the man and added his own compliments.

Morgan then told them that he'd eaten rabbit regularly when he'd been with the circus, and made a joke at which only Veronica laughed – not because it was funny, but because of her husband's fondness for the animals.

'Where do you keep 'em, then, these rabbits and pigeons?'

'Doves. Rabbits and doves.'

'Okay. Rabbits and doves.'

'There's a yard at the back of the theatre, out by one of the delivery areas. The manager keeps an eye on them. They're all quite happy and well fed.'

'No they're not. They're kept in tiny cramped baskets with barely room to turn round,' Veronica said, and carried on eating.

'They're not that small, love. You can't let them go running all over the place, can you? They're perfectly happy.' Derek looked around the table. Everyone except Morgan either nodded or smiled in agreement.

'Going to rain later,' Norman said, sensing the tension and wanting to change the subject.

'That's the forecast,' Derek added quickly.

'Tiny wicker baskets about this high,' Veronica continued, regardless, indicating the height of the baskets with her knife above the table.

Derek tried to ignore her.

'You were saying about work,' Veronica said, diverting the conversation back towards Rita, waiting until she had her mouth full of food. Rita nodded and tried to smile and chew simultaneously. Before she could speak, Morgan said: 'I saw a poster once in Derby or Leicester or somewhere for a stripper called "Randy Rita". That's not you, is it? He knew perfectly well that it wasn't.

'Oh no.' Rita tried to laugh, embarrassed, her denial sounding too much like an admission.

'Don't call them strippers any more,' Norman interrupted, largely for the benefit of Alice but also out of a misplaced sense of chivalry towards Rita. 'Exotic Dancers. Am I right?'

Rita said he was, and Norman smiled at each of the three women in the room. The ensuing silence was followed by the banging of cutlery as meals were finished.

'What's the difference, then?' Veronica asked.

'Difference?' Derek said, knowing full well what she meant.

'Between strippers and exotic dancers.'

Derek smiled apologetically at Rita. There was, of course, no difference: a stripper was a dancer who took off her clothes and an exotic dancer was a stripper who danced. Everyone knew there was no difference but everyone, for their own reasons, wanted to hear what she had to say. Everyone except Alice, who walked around the table collecting their plates.

'They're just names,' Rita said. 'Just names to describe the act, that's all.' She wanted to defend what she did, what she was; she wanted to tell them – to tell Veronica, to mind her own fucking business. A hand took her plate and she turned to acknowledge Alice.

' 'Course it is,' Norman said, obeying a signal from his wife, but not entirely certain if this agreed with what Rita had just said.

Morgan began humming again and tapping his spoon against his saucer.

Veronica turned to Norman and said that she'd like to see the photo of the diseased rabbits if it was no bother.

'No bother at all,' he assured her, pleased at her interest.

As predicted, it began to rain, and at half past six Derek and Veronica, Rita and Morgan left the warmth of the living room to prepare for their departure for the theatre.

In their bedroom the Priestleys argued and, at the wall, Morgan listened. Rita, too, heard their voices, and smiled at her own small victory.

'Any good?' Devlin nodded to the paperback lying in his mother's lap. He made no effort to sound interested but his words served to break the long silence between them.

The old woman stopped staring at the glass panel of the paraffin heater at her feet and looked up at her son and then at the description of the book on its back cover. He watched her and pulled a face as she began to read.

'This girl, whose un— unrequited love leads her on a journey towards a deeper understanding of herself and the man . . .'

But Devlin wasn't listening. He had asked about the book in the same way that he would ask what she had prepared for his tea or how she had spent her day. This was the limit of their dry intercourse.

'You want to get that fixed,' he interrupted, nodding at the paraffin heater. 'It stinks.' The heat rising from its brown enamel funnel rippled the air. There was no gas laid to their dilapidated chalet home, only electricity, and that was too expensive and ineffective, its warmth abandoning the small room through the poorly tiled walls and felt roof.

'Stinks,' he repeated. 'And all this condensation.' He pointed to the window and the lace curtains which clung to it with the damp. 'You'll have an accident one day – knock it over or something when I'm out. Then what? The whole place will be up in flames in minutes. And everything in it.' He turned away to inspect the contents of a saucepan, carrying it to the table where a single plate was set. 'I won't be back until turned eleven tonight,' he said, poured the food from the pan and ate whatever it might have been.

'Irish stew,' his mother said. She looked back to the heater, suddenly frightened at the prospect of a fire in which she and all her worthless belongings would be consumed. Why did he

36

say such things to her? Why did he frighten her like this?

'Eleven?' she asked out loud, half remembering what he had said.

Devlin nodded. She disgusted him. He turned his fork, letting its contents fall back to his plate with a splash.

She watched him and smiled. It was all a game: he was playing a game with her. He loved her, really, loved her too much to ever leave her. He was a good-looking man and could have had his pick of all the local girls. He told her so himself. The book slid from her lap and down her legs to the floor. She watched as it moved slowly along her thick stockings and over the bandage which covered her calf. It landed on the floor by the cupboard where they kept the paraffin. The door was open and she could see the plastic holders and their blue contents lined up under the sink.

Devlin ate his meal. A skin of white fat had formed around his plate like ice on a shallow puddle. On the chalet roof the drumming of the rain increased. Switching on the light he destroyed any impression of warmth the room might have had and his mother flinched, shielding her eyes from the stark fluorescent glare. She turned back to the ring of blue flames and tried to retrieve her book, sitting sharply upright at the pain of bending.

Devlin watched her and finished his mug of tea before telling her she ought to stop reading such rubbish, that it wasn't written for people like her.

'Only second-hand,' she said contritely, adding the name of the neighbour who brought her the books from a stall on the market and returned them against the cost of others a week later. 'A pound a week's not much. A pound a week for four. That's not a lot, Malcolm.'

Devlin did not answer. He smoked a cigarette, knocking the ash on to his plate. Through the window he saw the white bullet of the lighthouse, the glow from its glass collar. It turned slowly. In the darkness, its beam flashed into the room every few seconds, freezing everything as if in a photograph. Past the building it ran like a searchlight over the rows of caravans and holiday chalets which stretched like enamel studs over the adjoining fields.

'Quarter past four. Spot on. You could set your watch by that light.' He looked at his own watch. In the distance he saw the lights of an empty bus returning from the lighthouse to the village. 'And there's the bus. Spot on.'

His mother smiled, mistaking his comments for conversation. He made the same remarks every day and she was always happy to hear them. Some days they were the only things he said to her. Some days she waited, counting the dark afternoon hours until four-fifteen when he would hold up his watch and speak. Sometimes he added that the watch had never lost a minute in the two years he had had it. To her, such accuracy meant nothing. He crossed to the window and drew the curtains back to watch the flashing light, timing the seconds between each burst. From the gutters the rain ran in a continuous stream on to the bare earth beside the brick supports of their home. 'It'll come in soon,' he said. They were the last words between them for half an hour.

Devlin sat beside his record player, choosing from his collection of records. He sang along with them, tapping his feet and banging his hands on the table as he sorted through the worn black discs. These, too, were bought second-hand from a stall on the market. The sound was distorted, but he turned it louder. She would never complain. When he had gone out for the evening she would sit in front of the television. He would turn it on for her before leaving and switch it off upon his return. She would watch without changing channels, and tomorrow she would tell him what she had seen.

Crossing the room, he retrieved her paperback and read for himself about the girl and her quest for True Love, closing it firmly before dropping it back into her lap.

'It's sex; that's what she's after,' he said from behind her. 'It's not love or romance or anything like that: it's sex. I bet they never write that on the cover, do they?'

He had said similar things before and, as then, she was too embarrassed to answer.

'Look at her. Just look at her face.' He flicked the flimsy cover and made her jump. She looked down to the heroine's face, her pink lips and brown cheeks.

'You can tell just by looking with most women. You can—' He stopped suddenly and she waited, fearing what he might be about to say, what he was thinking. She felt the sudden rush of cold against her back as he opened the back door.

'Malcolm, what—?'

'Shut up!'

He stood in the doorway, his shadow stretching ahead of him over the wet grass, his arms resting on either side of the frame. Then he shut the door and knelt beside her to adjust the flames of the heater.

'There's somebody over on the camp,' he said, 'moving around in one of the chalets. A tramp, or maybe kids. I saw a light.'

She wanted to know more, to be reassured. She turned to look but saw nothing except the vague white forms crowding over the fields in the distance.

'Just a tramp bedding down for the night,' he said. 'Nothing for you to worry about.'

Picking up his coat and gloves he switched on the television and turned out the light.

Alone in the darkness, the old woman watched a comedian telling jokes, listening for any noise above the sound of his voice and the studio applause. But she heard nothing except the rain, and saw nothing except the blinding beam of the lighthouse as it swept over her home and in through the window.

Known Facts: Tracey Morton left number 17 Queensway Drive a little before or after ten minutes to seven on the evening of Thursday, the twenty-ninth of October. The walk to 31 Cranbrook Terrace, the home of Adele Shaw, her best friend, would ordinarily have taken little over ten minutes. She had arranged to be there at seven. Between leaving home and the eventual discovery of her body fifty-seven days later on the twenty-fourth of December, her whereabouts remained unknown and she was believed missing as opposed to dead.

Each year many thousands of similarly aged girls leave their homes, but the proportion later discovered to have been murdered – as opposed to permanently missing, 'Whereabouts Unknown' – is small enough to support the police in their initial response. This, of course, is no consolation to the missing girl's family.

Tracey's ten-minute journey had been re-enacted but, conditions being what they were, little or nothing was expected to be gained by the exercise. Nothing was.

Tracey's father, mother, brothers and sisters had been watching television as she picked her way through them across the

39

crowded room. Her young brothers hit at her legs and ankles as she stepped over them. On the television, a racing driver was being interviewed, and accordingly the boys made racing-car noises and ran their flat palms over the carpet.

In four hours it is possible to travel a considerable distance, and assuming Tracey's intentions had been to run away from home, those four hours achieved an exaggerated significance in the eyes of the police.

The two constables who arrived in the patrol car repeated that there was no cause for alarm and asked her mother to repeat the details she had already given over the phone. She was interrupted by her husband, who shouted and gestured angrily towards the men. They asked him the colour of his daughter's eyes and he did not know.

Afterwards, when the two policemen had gone, her mother sat in the kitchen and began to cry.

It was as the constables waited in their car that the message that Tracey had never arrived at the home of her friend was broadcast to them, thus confirming that she had been missing for over four and a half hours. The driver logged the message at ten minutes to midnight. On the bonnet, the frost had melted in circles with the heat of the engine. Along the street other cars began to whiten.

According to the pathologist's report, written fifty-nine days later, death had been caused by strangulation. The leg-warmer still wrapped around Tracey's neck had, apparently, been used to continue the pressure after she was already dead, which led the inquest to conclude that she had died within a short period of her breathing being obstructed, ten or possibly twenty seconds. It also led the police to conclude that her killer had not known she was dead and that he had continued to apply pressure long after it was necessary to do so. There was also reason to believe that she was already dead when sexually assaulted.

The report also noted that her knickers had not been replaced, and that her vagina and upper thighs showed signs of considerable bruising. There were signs of her having been bitten on her breasts and upper arms. On her neck were the frozen bruises of her strangulation, and on her arms and legs the scratches of her struggle. From the blood still congealed in these wounds, the coroner was able to estimate the likely passage of time between the wounds being inflicted and the time of her death. Again it could be measured in seconds rather than minutes.

The killer had remained undetected by any third party for the duration of the time taken to attack, kill and assault the girl, and the body was then carried or dragged into the adjoining allotments, screened from outside by a tall, untidy hedge. The killer had also been careful to collect her shoes and handbag and take these too.

Inside the allotments the body had been half buried beneath a mound of loose soil and rotting vegetable matter. The mound, it should be noted, was of a considerable size – being communal – and existed prior to Tracey's burial within it. In overall shape and size nothing changed with the addition of the girl's body. It was not, one might guess, until after her killer had left that the debris covering her feet had fallen away to expose them.

Later that night it had rained, which in turn froze, compacting the material even further, settling it into the spaces around the body.

3

Vincent walked from the simple shelter which marked the bus terminus to the Happy Cliffs Caravan Camp, where he intended to find somewhere to stay for the night. The journey took almost an hour along a narrow road which rose and fell over the uneven ground and along which the wind and rain drove straight in from the sea. He tasted the salt on his lips and felt the rain on his closed eyes. After only a few minutes his clothes were coated with water which formed into droplets, falling from his cuffs and nose.

He would have waited in the shelter had the bus not stood there as the driver counted out his change. Vincent cursed his luck and walked away past the lines of empty boarding houses and small hotels towards where the fields of caravans stretched down to the cliff edge. He was alone and felt considerably more conspicuous than he had done in the town. He read the names of the hotels and, in their small gardens, he saw rusted anchors and concrete cast sundials and white metal furniture dripping with the rain. He came to where the street lights ended and ahead of him was only darkness and the sea.

Entering the caravan camp by the main entrance would, he mistakenly believed, have attracted attention to what he was doing. Nothing went into the camp in winter except the tractor and trailer which took in the men and equipment to dig new drains or prepare more sites, squeezing the holiday homes closer and closer together. He climbed instead through a tight boundary hedge and followed the line of an untidy field to where the caravans began. From a rise in the ground he looked over the camp. Line after line of caravans, all set out in rows like cream and white shoe boxes, all empty, all rocking in the wind. Between them he saw the few lines of weatherboard and stucco chalets, laid out like bricks in the half light. At the centre of the camp was a children's playground, deserted now, the sandpit blown empty and the swings chained to their frames like vines. Through the window of the empty clubhouse he saw the bar stripped of bottles and the tables lined with chairs – the scene illuminated only by the fading afternoon light.

He examined a line of caravans before deciding that a chalet would be easier to break into. Choosing one, he drew his cuff over his fist and smashed a small window. The sound of breaking glass filled the entire camp for the seconds it took to fall and shatter.

From inside the chalet, he had an unobstructed view over an empty field to the top of the cliffs and the sea beyond. He stared out and considered the apparent hopelessness of his position. He thought of Alice and of her warm home, its colourful carpets and wallpaper, its walls hung with pictures of children and horses, its shelves lined with brass and porcelain and glass ornaments. He thought also of Norman, of his contrived jokes and predictable remarks.

There was running water in the chalet, but neither gas nor electricity. His clothes were wet and he was hungry. In the kitchen he found a drawer of cutlery and a cupboard full of assorted crockery and glasses. On the shelf he found six place mats with assorted views of London. Using a pile of yellowing newspapers he lit a fire in a metal waste bin. The flames lit up the small room in which he sat but did little to warm him. It did not occur to him then that someone might see the flickering light.

Next he searched the bedrooms but found nothing, not even a pillow case with which to dry himself. Sitting at the table he closed his eyes and knew that things must get better the next day.

The rain began to fall more heavily, and then to drip through the ceiling with an irregular rhythm. He found the leak and placed a cup beneath it. (It was that cup, along with the broken window and burnt residue in the bin which was later to provide the police searching for the missing girl with the evidence to suggest that someone had spent one night at least in the empty chalet.)

Under the window grew orange and brown fungus, spreading in beads beneath the saturated woodwork.

Vincent looked out and saw nothing but the caravans running in lines to the brow of the hill and beyond. In summer children flew kites from that hill. He knew because he had done it himself.

From the smaller window at the rear of the chalet, he looked back to the road along which he had come. He saw the light-house and the line of chalets in which people lived all year round. In them he saw lights, and rising from their chimneys he could

43

make out smoke. 'Kennels,' he said to himself, repeating the word over and over simply to hear his own voice and to fill the empty room with sound. In one chalet he saw a door open, a block of light appear and then the outline of a tiny figure. He watched and then turned away.

At nine o'clock he smoked his last cigarette, burning the packet and reviving the brief, flickering shadows which climbed the walls, filling the room with a smell which followed him to sleep an hour later curled inside the thin carpet.

The slender pincers of the harbour closed around a basin of shining mud, through which several drains made their way to the sea. Marking them were buoys, their pennants flapping vigorously. The mud was criss-crossed with a lacework pattern of gull tracks as the birds scavenged, fighting over what might have been thrown down from above or abandoned by the tide.

Rita pressed herself into the corner of the wooden bench set into a recess in the harbour wall. She could hear and see the wind as it blew over the enclosed scene, but where she sat she was relatively free from its effects. She pushed her hands into her pockets and folded them into her groin.

The few remaining fishing boats sat at awkward angles, their anchors, buoys and restraining ropes trailing slackly away into the mud. Around them were crowded the smaller rowing boats, hired out for fishing or pleasure trips during the summer, each with a woman's name painted across its stern. She searched for her own but could not find it. This did not surprise her: she could not imagine anyone wanting to risk their lives on the open sea in a boat called Rita. She was afternoon drunk and thus given to such feelings. She remembered a joke about why boats were named after women – something about if a boat sank then it was always better to be buried in a woman than . . . She forgot the rest.

On a nearby blackboard were chalked the times of low and high tides and the condition of the sea. She read them but they meant nothing to her. Above her, and towards the centre of the town, she saw the distant shapes of afternoon shoppers as they crossed brightly lit windows. She saw people riding in buses and the flashing lights of zebra crossings. In an hour she would be able to make her way back to the guest house and turn on the electric bar heater in her room. There were days when she did not even want to leave the house, but being alone with either Alice or Norman still made her feel awkward. Apart from which, there were Alice's rules about vacating the rooms and Norman's remarks on the cost of electricity. On the days when there were neither rehearsals nor matinées at the theatre, the hours between the closing of the bars and her return home seemed to Rita to be the longest and coldest of the day.

Besides her work at the theatre she had an engagement for the following Sunday lunchtime. The folded letter from her ex-agent was in her handbag, the booking in a Working Men's Club twenty minutes from where she was staying. 'Good Luck,' the man had written, waiving any fee and not even signing his name on the headed notepaper with its grinning and frowning masks.

Along the curving wall of the Promenade she saw the figure of a man as he leant against the railings, looking over the sea towards its invisible horizon. Beyond him she saw the first, irregular flashes of the lighthouse. The man raised both hands, stretching before thrusting them back into his pockets. She saw the explosion of sparks as his cigarette hit the stone wall and vanished. A woman paused by the harbour steps before turning away.

Morgan sat where he could not be seen by any other members of the staff of the supermarket. He smoked and held a plastic beaker of coffee between his hands. Occasionally, at the other end of one of the fridges, the white-coated butchers would slide out a muslin-wrapped carcase and carry it over their shoulders into the butchery room. Morgan saw the blue stamps and the balls of fat which coated the legs of beef.

Morgan sat alone because some of the women had objected to his presence in the staff canteen, which they considered their own. The butchers had their own table and kettle which they shared with the man from the greengrocery department. The Wines and Cigarettes man had his tea taken to him in his kiosk, and the shelf fillers and warehousemen sat around in other hidden corners stealing chocolate and playing cards.

Christmas was less than five weeks away and the store was already geared towards the increase in sales. Streams of crêpe paper stretched above the crowded shelves, balloons hung above the fridges in suggestive designs, and from the Tannoy came the muted hymns and carols of all Christmases.

The women had not said in so many words that Morgan was not welcome in their canteen but they always seemed to break off their conversations as he strutted in, his green nylon coat trailing almost to his ankles, its sleeves rolled to thick bunches at his elbows. Once he overheard one of them saying she wouldn't mind taking him home for use as a garden ornament. 'And for one or two other things!' another woman had shouted, making them all laugh and Morgan seek out somewhere else to take his tea breaks.

Like everyone else in the store, Morgan had no inhibitions about stealing. He stole chocolates and cakes from the shelves, cooked meat and cheese from the fridges. On one occasion he had stolen a large tin of salmon from one of the boxes in the canyon of packing cases amongst which he worked. He ate the flakes of meat with his fingers, licking at the oil as it ran down his wrists and arms. It was the first time he had tasted salmon, and ever since he had taken a tin a day, saving it until he was alone in his retreat with boxes stacked against the door to prevent anyone from coming in and finding him.

Alone, he thought about Veronica. He thought, too, about her husband and about Alice and Norman. Sometimes he thought about Rita, but there was something about her that stopped him from being envious in the way he envied most people. He saw in her someone in a similar position to his own, trapped as inevitably as he was within his joke of a body.

He thought, too, about the circus, about its collapse and his entry into a world unprepared for him. He still had a small black and white photograph of his midget parents on their wedding day, him in his cut-off suit and her in a lace dress she had made herself, standing waist high to the semi-circle of performers behind them. The picture made him want to swear and to curse them for what they had done and for the inevitable and predictable course of his life ahead.

Norman pulled the green rubber waders up to his chest. The buckles were fastened from behind by two of his colleagues who told jokes about frogs and made croaking sounds.

'Very funny,' Norman whispered, but could say nothing more because of the small group of his superior officers who stood beside the car parked at the edge of the black pool into which he was about to wade. The more junior policemen discussed the possibility of finding the girl's body and getting back to something warmer by lunchtime.

At eight o'clock it was still not fully light and the blue spinning lights cut strange patterns over the surface of the municipal tip. Beside the entrance stood an ambulance.

The only real light over the entire scene came from the open door of the watchman's Portakabin, through the windows of which a collage of check sheets, invoices and pin-ups of naked women were clearly visible. The man stood in the doorway and watched as the police prepared to search, manoeuvring their cars over the firmer surfaces, their headlights bouncing across the uneven ground. He grinned to himself as those who had not had the sense to wear wellingtons stepped out on to the sodden surface and swore helplessly as they slashed at the loose litter with the poles they carried. He shouted warnings to them about the compaction of the refuse and about the frost and pointed to the yellow bulldozer parked beside his hut, but no one listened.

'Right, sergeant.' The man in the car shouted the words and wound up the window.

Norman half-saluted, hearing the muffled laughter of the two constables who stood on the opposite side of the pool, and who held the rope attached to his waist.

He took two steps forward and sank to his chest in the clinging black liquid. 'No smoking,' he heard someone shout, and turned in time to see them laughing and pointing in his direction. He shivered as the cold seeped through the waders. With his pole he stirred the liquid ahead of him. The surface moved in viscous ripples which quickly faded. His wake closed behind him, and when he stopped moving the surface of the pool became perfectly calm, giving off only a faint smell of oil in the freezing air. A job for an officer, they had said, and he had volunteered.

Norman pushed his pole, hardly daring to move forward, feeling the unseen ground beneath his feet give as he swayed from side to side. He poked and prodded, catching his breath at each obstacle and seeing his name on the report as the officer responsible for the discovery of the girl's body.

An unattended radio repeated its message and one of the men holding the rope walked gingerly back to his car, sitting sideways in the seat to reply. Norman stopped. Others turned to watch and listen. The man in the car shouted, waved and shook his head. Windows were re-wound and faces turned back to Norman at the centre of the pool.

Norman watched them and said 'Damn' beneath his breath, angry at the unnecessary cold and discomfort, but still pleased by the prospect that of them all, he was the one most likely to find the girl.

In an hour, when the light improved, they would begin to search systematically, crossing the ground in a staggered line like beaters trying to flush the body from where it lay hidden. But almost three weeks had passed since the girl had gone missing and the surface of the tip had been repeatedly covered and compacted. If they were going to uncover anything then they would have to look much deeper than the frozen crust through which they now prepared to pick.

The gatekeeper watched them, explaining what was happening as officiously as possible to the dustcart drivers who began to arrive demanding to unload. What girl? they wanted to know, angry at the delay. What about their bonus schemes? Why couldn't they leave it until the weekend?

In the pool Norman moved from side to side. In parts a crust of solid grey foam had collected, breaking ahead of him like ice beneath the bows of a ship. He prodded the pieces, lifting them clear of the liquid on his pole. Someone shouted to ask him what he had found and the headlights of a car shone across the black surface.

But Norman wasn't listening; instead he was thinking about the pictures he had seen of dinosaurs struggling in pools of pitch, screaming and roaring (he supposed) as they sank deeper and deeper into extinction. He remembered the mastodons and the woolly mammoths frozen into the Siberian ice.

Around him the others formed into parties and began testing the ground and fastening chains to the dogs which strained excitedly at the prospect of being set loose on this kaleidoscope of smells and tastes.

In a fortnight the police would hold their annual Christmas dinner and their professional cares and anxieties would be forgotten. The words 'Annual' and 'Christmas' were printed on the tickets. Even policemen needed to let their hair down, the Chief Constable said. They were only human – more human, in fact, than most of those with whom they came daily into contact. (That was another of his jokes.)

Norman stood like a statue in a fountain at the centre of the pool, and in the distance the orange sun began to rise.

At home, Alice put away the last of her breakfast dishes and turned to watch the man standing beside her rear gate. He was looking up at the house, searching the windows. He saw her and hesitated, and as he drew back the latch on the gate, she opened her mouth to shout.

4

Roland Trotter, Theatre Manager (impresario was the term he preferred, but did not fully understand and thus seldom used), reclined in his reclining chair, chequered red and gold, and looked out over the masts (stripped for the most part of rigging) which broke the skyline running left and right from his own extensive lawn. As he did so he thought back to the time when the town had been the . . . what was it? 'The Bustling Home of Maritime Commerce.' And as he sat thinking, he drank from his heavy glass and looked once again at the cheap brochure which had arrived in that morning's post. It was from an enterprising local builder who promised to install an Authentic-style Sailing Ship-type Mast in any suitable garden for less than the price of an ornamental pond.

All around Roland Trotter's bungalow other, older masts rose from green lawns as though a whole fleet of ships had been sunk there, presided over now by plaster gnomes with ruddy cheeks who stalked the crazy-paved patios and reconstituted-stone cherub bird baths.

Roland Trotter wanted a mast. 'Look out over your own mast, your own reminder of a Rich and Colourful Seafaring Heritage.'

Heritage. As a member of the Civic Society it was a word he enjoyed using. Already he possessed various other varnished, polished and largely ornamental artefacts of maritime history which, if pieced back together, would probably constitute a reasonably seaworthy bungalow. But a mast with rigging. Rigging – that would make all the difference. Rigging and flags, like at the coastguard station. Already he saw the mast rising up from the centre of his expensively striped lawn. Perhaps he could even change the name of the bungalow to something a little more nautical.

Excited at the prospect of having his own mast, he began to swivel in his chair, tilting it further back into one of the dozen positions promised by the manufacturer.

The silence was broken only by the sound of his fat children stampeding along the hallway into the kitchen. He heard his eldest daughter scream and then the sound of something more solid as her eleven stones came into contact with a door.

In addition to being despised by his own children, Roland Trotter considered himself to be a man much misunderstood by the world at large – a pillar of society not yet girdled with the wreaths of civic honours he deserved, or had at least paid for. Pouring another drink he turned once again to his lawn. Beyond it, out from the town, a charcoal-coloured cloud dragged itself over the grey sea.

As he watched, two figures crossed his view, moving slowly along the public footpath which ran past the bottom of his garden (a footpath which he and the others of the Residents Association had tried to have removed). He stared hard and recognised Malcolm Devlin and his mother as they made their way home, using the path as a short cut between the bus terminus and their dilapidated chalet.

Thursday, no matinée. Devlin's mother walked behind her son, carrying a shopping bag, appearing to limp. Devlin stopped and waited for her. Ahead of them the low dark shapes of the chalets lined the road, running up and over the rise towards the lighthouse.

There was something about Devlin that bothered Roland Trotter: something about the way he refused to respond to any friendly advance or even to make the simplest conversation beyond that which was absolutely necessary.

The door banged open and his son and eldest daughter ran in, stopping when they saw him and turning to each other with a look of disappointment. Clapping the crumbs from their hands on to the carpet, they turned and ran out, leaving him to guess at what they had hoped to find. When he looked back towards the sea, Devlin and his mother had gone and the first flashes of the light gathered momentum and swept over his garden.

He looked again at the brochure in his lap and read the words *Marie Celeste* and *Flying Dutchman*. The sea beckoned. To-morrow he would ring the builder.

On the day Vincent left the Happy Cliffs Caravan Camp and walked the four miles back to town, the crows lined the telegraph wires like the heavy notes of a funeral march arranged along a stave. He looked up and saw them, clapped his hands and swore loudly, immediately embarrassed by the sound of his voice as it echoed along the deserted road. The cold strengthened his resolve to see Alice, and as he walked he practised what he would say to her, trying to imagine her response. He would ask to stay with her until New Year before returning to Wolverhampton to take up once again with Maureen and the children. Of course, he did not know then of the alternative arrangements already being made by Maureen, nor of the succession of lorry-driver lodger-lovers arriving nightly at their former home.

Vincent's back and legs ached from the cold floor of the chalet. He looked down at his creased and dirty suit and knew that there were better ways to make an appearance.

On the outskirts of the town he passed the large and conspicuously ornate homes of its wealthier citizens, its councillors, bank managers and businessmen, its fringe of retired people, sitting out their days in bungalows with well-tended gardens, secure in the knowledge that life and its problems lay behind them and all that lay ahead was a comfortable decline into old age, senility and death. At one of these houses, he watched as three fat children stood beside a coughing car, banging on its doors and shouting complaints to the man inside who tried unsuccessfully to coax it into life.

Approaching the town centre, his resolve began to melt. He rehearsed his lines and tried not to look at the people who passed him on their way to work.

Nine o'clock. If Norman was on the day shift, then Alice would be alone. She would cook him a hot breakfast, give him cigarettes and sit him in front of the fire.

Arriving at the line of guest houses, he counted along them in an effort to pick out his sister's home.

The Sunday lunchtime engagement had been Rita's first work as a stripper for over three months. Money in the hand always excited her, always made her feel worth something – in this case, thirty pounds for two appearances.

The first performance had been well-received in the half-filled room, payment immediately afterwards, congratulations from the Entertainments Secretary, one arm round her shoulders, the other slapping her knee where her dressing gown fell open. He filled the small room with smoke, his wide frame blocking the doorway, bending to avoid the warm pipes which crossed it at head height.

'Lovely, darling. Just what we needed. Another show as good as that one and I think we might be able to work out something a bit more . . . shall we say a bit more regular?' He had a strong local accent and wiped his lips as he spoke. He raised his eyebrows, his grip on her knee tightening as he waited for her answer. She smiled and drew together her dressing gown, pulling the cord into her soft waist. Only the money in her hand made her tolerate his lewdness.

'What do you say, love? Like to come in on a more regular basis? We generally have a Men Only every other Thursday, and we're always on the look out for Sunday lunchtime spots.'

As he spoke, Rita watched herself in the mirror.

'I'm not sure. I don't live locally.' She saw the moving mouth and pursed her lips.

'We used to get 'em in on a regular basis, every weekend nearly. But that was before well, before the change in management. And what with one thing and another . . .'

The man was still talking. She saw his bulging shirt and trousers. He hadn't used the word 'stripper' yet. They seldom did.

She turned from the mirror to face him and ask for a cigarette. This he interpreted as a positive response and gave her one. She thanked him and said that the lights in the Concert Room were too strong, that they blinded her.

'Can't have that, can we?' he laughed, promising to do something about them.

She waited for him to leave, and he waited for an answer to his proposition. On a hanger behind the door hung her dress, swaying slightly and reminding them both of her nakedness beneath the loose dressing gown.

It was quarter to one. She had another three-quarters of an hour to wait. Free drinks had been promised, but these, she knew, seldom amounted to much.

'We could put you on for a full half hour if you like,' he said.

'Suit yourself.' She was immune now to the man's promises and dropped the money on to the dressing table, drawing her fingers through its dust of powders.

'We could run to an extra tenner. What do you think? Half an hour?'

53

She shrugged. There seemed little real possibility of her stretching over half an hour what she could accomplish in a minute when alone, or ten when paid. And there was the audience to consider: by then they would be different men from those tempted to stare and whistle at her first appearance. By then they would be drunk and brave, and half an hour was a long time to stand undressed in front of such a crowd.

'We had a woman with a snake at one time. Big black bugger, black and yeller.' He smiled at the thought. 'And another time we had one who brought all these costumes – nurse, schoolkid, that sort of thing.' He looked as if he hoped she too might have some such novelty to offer.

Rita screwed her cigarette into the ashtray. A knocking sounded along the pipes, emphasising the silence.

The man turned to leave. 'Right, then, I'll— Oh, you won't be leaving the dressing room, will you? Not that we don't trust you, you understand, but we've had one or two in the past who've taken advantage of the, er . . .' – he nodded gravely at the memory – 'who've taken it upon themselves to bugger off halfway through their booking. Not that anybody's accusing you, mind, but some of the members got a bit upset.' He held up his palms, smiling and waiting for her assurance, which she gave with a single nod.

'And then there's the bar. We, er . . . We don't generally like the performers to go into the bar. Sometimes leads to, er, to bad feelings amongst the members . . . But we'll send someone in with a drink. If there's anything in particular you want, you've only to ask. Tell them I said you'd to ask.' He paused, waiting for her answer. 'So I'll tell them not to bother with the full half hour, shall I? Or what do you think? Shall we give it a go? I honestly think that—'

'Oh, for Christ's sake,' she shouted, her patience with the man gone. 'Tell them what the fucking hell you like. Just get out!'

The man stopped and returned to stand behind her, staring at her in the mirror, his hands gripping the back of her chair, his knuckles touching her shoulders.

'Look, love, there's no need to get fuckin' stroppy with me. I'm only trying to be friendly.' His voice had changed, made harsh by the re-emergence of his accent. 'We've had your sort in here before and—'

'So you said.'

'— if you think we have to put up with this kind of behaviour then you've got another think coming. I was doing you a favour, love. It's no skin off my nose. It's money in your pocket, not mine.'

'Here,' she shouted, standing to face him and realising for the first time that she was slightly taller than he was. 'Here! Here's your money: you go up and take your fucking trousers off and wave your cock around for them all to have a good look at. Here! Go on – take it!' He raised his arm as though to hit her. She saw him falter and said softly, 'Go on, then.' The man lowered his arm and crossed back to the door.

'And send some cigarettes in, will you, there's a good lad. I'm sure the *members* can bear the cost of twenty fags. And if not, I'll stop up there an extra two minutes to pay for them. How will that suit? God forbid that I should do anybody out of anything they were entitled to.'

The man turned, banged his head on the low pipes and swore.

'You want to get shut of some of them airs and graces, you do,' he said. 'Do you want to know why? I'll tell you, shall I? 'Cos you're a fuckin' has-been, that's why. A fuckin' has-been. And don't bother coming back here for work because I can promise you one thing – you'll not work in any of our affiliated clubs again.'

'How ever will I survive?' She began to laugh. The man waited by the door, his hand tightening on the handle.

'Tell you what,' she said. 'Here's fifteen quid back. We'll forget about the second performance, shall we? You can go out and explain to the aud— to the precious *members* that there's been some misunderstanding. They'll like that, I'm sure. Go on, tell them that I wasn't really what you expected. Perhaps next weekend you could get a string quartet in, or Sooty or something like that.' She laughed again as his face fell, trying to assess the seriousness of her threat. She began to count the money, scaring him even further. He turned without speaking and slammed out of the room. She watched in the mirror, not knowing whether to laugh or cry, whether she had won or lost.

Now she had half an hour to wait. She watched in the mirror as her dress swung in slow arcs behind the door, reminding her unaccountably of a long-forgotten girlhood dream of becoming a ballet dancer. In the harsh light the room became suddenly cold and she rubbed her bare arms.

Derek sat at the table. It was mid-afternoon, and apart from himself, Veronica and Alice, the house was empty. Veronica was upstairs, and from the kitchen came the sound of Alice moving crockery and opening cupboard doors. On his lap sat a large, fluffy, yellow bird; his arm through its neck, his hand opening and closing the beak. The children loved it. 'Ossie' the Ostrich. 'Ostrich' was inaccurate (as Norman had been quick to point out), but no one else seemed bothered. On stage, the bird's head turned from side to side, its stuffed red legs hanging limply beneath his elbow.

'And what about you, Ossie? Have you ever had a dream about flying away from all this, flying home to a place beyond a rainbow and living in the sun on a tropical island?' These were lines from the pantomime. (Again, only Norman had pointed out that ostriches could not fly.)

On stage there was no need for Derek to disguise the movement of his mouth. The children watched Ossie, not him.

'*Fly away. Who, me?*' A higher voice, his teeth together.

Alice looked round the door to see who was talking. Seeing the bird, she commented on how realistic it looked.

Derek sat at the table, the bird's legs crossed over his own, his mouth hidden by the synthetic yellow fur of its head.

'*And how about you, Alice? Have you ever wanted to escape, to shake everything off and fly away to a land where worries and troubles aren't allowed?*' The bird's head cocked in expectation of an answer.

'We can but dream, I suppose,' she replied, sitting opposite him at the table, unsure of whether to address her answer to Derek or the bird, which looked from one to the other, opening its beak wide before falling dead on to the table.

'It's part of the act, see,' he said, not needing to explain, but wanting to break the silence.

'Oh, yes. Well, it's very realistic.' She answered him for the same reason. 'Veronica upstairs, is she? Tired, I expect.'

The bird lifted its head, nodded and fell back to the table with a knock.

'Where is it you're going after here? Anything lined up?'

' "Lined up"?' He smiled at the phrase. 'Once, you know, we were all set to do a full summer season, May to September, on a cruise liner. A cruise liner, all in – board, meals everything – the Mediterranean.'

Alice nodded, smiled and said, 'Nice, the Mediterranean.'

'We didn't, of course. Never got any further than buying the luggage.'

'Oh, what a shame. You'd have enjoyed that. All that sun, and the sea.'

Derek agreed with her, lifting the bird to his face and stroking its yellow neck. 'No, we've got nothing special lined up. Back down to the Midlands, I suppose. Back round the clubs. There's not the special party trade there used to be – stags, private dinners, sports bookings, that sort of thing.'

Alice concentrated on the bird, embarrassed now by his tone.

'And so we've come to this,' he concluded. 'This and kids' parties. Homes, hospitals . . .'

'It brings a lot of pleasure,' Alice said, not knowing what else to say.

'It was Veronica, you see. On account of Veronica that we got most of the private bookings, the Working Men's and such. She was younger then. I suppose we both were. She used to dance and—' He stopped and looked across to where Alice waited. 'Times change, I suppose.'

She nodded, relieved that he had not finished what he might have been about to say.

'Isn't that right, Ossie? Times change, needs must and all that.'

The bird looked at each of them, as if uncertain of the answer expected from it.

'*A land across the rainbow where the sun shines all day and troubles aren't allowed,*' it said, and fell limply into his lap.

Alice smiled. They were back where they had started. 'Norman likes birds,' she said. 'Knows most of them, knows their nests and things like that. What they eat, eggs, that sort of thing. Not just birds from this country, either. America, Africa. Birds of Paradise, lovely, all colours. He has some pictures.' She pointed to the cabinet in which the books were kept.

They both now heard Veronica descending the stairs. Alice went back to the kitchen and Derek pulled the bird to the table as she entered the room.

Veronica blew smoke towards the ceiling, her head level with the small wooden plaque asking guests to respect the wishes of others when smoking. She looked at Derek, at the frosted glass of the kitchen door, and at the bird rising to life as his arm squeezed through it. Picking up a magazine, she sat in Norman's chair, pulling it towards the fire and turning up the short blue flames. Derek said she ought not to tamper with the fire.

'You just see to that stupid bloody bird and I'll see to myself. All right?' She opened the magazine and began to read, holding it between her husband and herself, tapping ash from her cigarette into the hearth at her feet. Derek took an ashtray and placed it beside her.

'Do you remember the time we nearly did that Mediterranean cruise?' he said.

'No.' She turned the page noisily to indicate that the conversation was over.

Derek threw the yellow bird at the table where it caught on a chair and hung upside-down.

'Temper, temper,' Veronica said and smiled coldly, blowing a fist of smoke towards him.

5

Since his arrival a fortnight ago Vincent, largely to appease Norman and establish his own position in this household of family and strangers, had done his utmost to appear to be doing his best to rehabilitate himself.

During the first week of his stay Norman had made his feelings clearly known, remaining just short of being openly aggressive towards his brother-in-law, indulging himself instead in restrained hostility of a type against which no one, least of all Alice, could complain. No one, in short, could accuse him of being unjust, and slowly the men had struck a balance, each testing himself against the other in the public arena of the house. Vincent, aware of his grudging acceptance by his brother-in-law, played upon the relationship to secure his position. In turn, Norman set out to prove that under his guidance and influence, Vincent would achieve his aim of rehabilitation. It became something of a personal challenge.

With the release of tension brought about by this unlikely truce, Alice's dormant fondness for her brother grew. They spoke about the past, and when they were alone together she indulged him with cakes and laughter, telling him not to take her husband too seriously.

The presence of the other guests helped in several ways to cushion the blow of Vincent's arrival – largely as a result of Norman's insistence that they should not be told of his past, of what he was ('Has been,' corrected Alice. 'Was. *Is*,' insisted Norman).

During the second week of his stay, Norman suggested that Vincent might like to meet Major Halifax. Major Halifax, Norman explained, was the chairman and leader of a group of local people (most of them council-connected or redundant dignitaries) who had formed the 'Friends of the Police Society'. The group had been created many years previously in an era of demands for community involvement and greater account-ability. Now the Friends had been relegated to attending Magistrates' Courts and reporting back to their members on the leniency of the police where youth was concerned.

Major Halifax had been a policeman of one sort or another all his life and had stated publicly his intention of dying in the service of his community. His own palatial and securely protected house on the outskirts of Marton lay three miles from the town, its outer walls dotted with bright red alarm boxes, its leaded windows and high beech hedges revealing nothing of what might be worth stealing. Unfortunately for the police, Major Halifax chose to make little distinction between the Kenyan bush over which he had presided for thirty years and the English seaside town in which he now lived.

An unsympathetic newspaper editor had once referred to the Friends as Vigilantes and Interfering Do-gooders. Via the intervention of one Friend and on the insistence of another, a retraction was promptly printed. The Good Work of the Friends had been conspicuously ignored ever since. The press ignored them, the police ignored them, and the public ignored them. Norman, however, did not: he saw a place for such a group, albeit a different one from that which they themselves had hoped to secure.

As well as being chairman of the Friends, Major Halifax was secretary of the local Civic Society, treasurer of the British Legion and a vocal participant of assorted other local societies, Masons included.

During that first fortnight in his sister's home, Vincent found the house even more claustrophobic than his prison cell had been, and it was only when he was alone with Alice that he felt completely secure. Together they spoke about his wife and children; about his past and his prospects for the future; about what he could have done and might have been; about the way circumstance and luck had conspired against him, leaving him without goals or direction. They were excuses, but Alice was prepared to believe them. She reassured him and, in that uncertain world, she was all he had and he depended upon her.

A week after his arrival a brief letter had arrived from Maureen, addressed to Alice and asking if he was there and what he thought he was playing at. What about her and the children? Was she expected to feed and clothe them on what she earned? She was still young and if he thought she was going to waste her time waiting until he came to his senses then he'd got another think coming. Darren had had German Measles but the rest of them were keeping well, discounting her headaches and back. A postscript to the letter said that if he wasn't with Alice then where could he be. She hoped that she and Norman were well. Best wishes for a Merry Christmas and a Happy New Year.

Alice showed the letter to Vincent whose heart sank as he read its ten, barely punctuated lines, despairing at the growing conspiracy which began to wrap itself around him and draw him back.

Alice had never liked Maureen and told him not to worry. Vincent fought back the impulse to defend his wife, but realising that such an impulse still existed gave him a strange sense of satisfaction, rekindling in him the faint hope of a reconciliation. What about the measles, wasn't it dangerous in a kid that age? Alice reassured him with a list of their own childhood ailments, ailments modern children knew nothing about. She made other comparisons, reviving more memories of happier times. He laughed and she joined him, holding each other and rocking on the sofa, the tray of tea and biscuits rattling on the table at their feet.

In the days that followed the letter, Vincent tried to find work, casual work where no records or references were required. He asked at the supermarket where Morgan worked; at the council offices, parks department and at several other large stores. No promises were made and only rarely were any details taken with an offer of contacting him if anything came up.

That night, the night after the arrival of the letter (never shown to Norman), Norman turned to Alice as they lay in bed and said: 'What with you and me and Major Halifax, and given that he's prepared to make a go of things, there's every chance that Vincent could make something of himself.' He then turned away to preclude any further discussion. Alice resented his patronising tone.

'Yes, Norman.' And she also turned away.

As he spoke, Tracey Morton's father nodded directly into the camera, leaning forward to talk into the microphone being held off-screen. Mid-way through his first sentence, a man wearing headphones waved his hand in front of the lens. A woman with a clipboard and a pen between her teeth walked towards Tracey's father, who was still speaking, looking from side to side, uncertain of what was happening. It was the third false start to the brief news item. His daughter had been missing exactly a month and this anniversary had promoted her disappearance into once again being a newsworthy item.

'. . . anything like it before. In fact, as far as her mother and – what? You want . . .?'

He stopped speaking as the woman led him away from the camera and explained to him the need to keep still when he spoke, no leaning towards the microphone; everybody would hear what he said. All right? He smiled, more flattered than rebuked.

'Nerves,' he explained. 'Not every day you're on the television, is it?' She, in fact, was, but she agreed with him. Next time it would be perfect.

Behind them the cameraman lifted his apparatus into position and shouted to her. She turned towards him and they shared an understanding look. The sound man pointed his microphone and held up his thumb. Beneath his cushioned headphones he heard nothing except the sound of Tracey's father coughing and clearing his throat.

'Mr Morton, it's been exactly a month since your daughter, Tracey, disappeared, and so far the police have had no success in tracing her and she has made no attempt to contact you. How do you feel after all this time? Do you still believe that she is safe and well and that she will one day return?'

'A month. Yes. Well, it's er . . . We've had no word, her mother and me. No word. And it's like I was saying earlier, she's always . . .'

He continued to talk as the cameraman swore and the woman stuck the pen back between her teeth. It was her way of remaining outwardly calm. Tracey's father, meanwhile, continued to explain and apologise for forgetting what they had rehearsed.

The interview was taking place on the street in front of the house in which Tracey had last been seen by her parents. Neighbours emerged, waving towards the camera every time it turned away from its subject.

'We really must get it right this time, Mr Morton. Much longer and we're not going to have the light. We really must try and get it all in one run. All we need is thirty seconds. I know it might seem like a lot, but we really must try. O.K.?'

Thirty seconds. A second for each day Tracey had been missing, dead and buried.

Her father smiled and apologised, pulling at his tie and taking an offered cigarette. His collar rubbed. The sound and cameramen walked into the road, smoking and swinging their arms in wide circles. The crowd asked when they could expect to see the interview on television.

'About two months at this rate,' the sound man said and both men laughed. The crowd smiled, uncertain of the joke.

'Right, Mr Morton. I ask about how you feel, about it being a month since . . . since . . .'

'Tracey.'

'Yes. Since Tracey disappeared. Okay? Got that? You just give me about ten seconds saying that you haven't heard from her and that you still have every confidence that she's okay and living somewhere else. Okay?'

'Every confidence and living somewhere else.'

'That's it. I mean, that is what you want to say, isn't it? Don't let me put the words into your mouth if it's not what you believe – not if you think she's been . . .'

Sensing that if he changed what he was going to say then the interview might be abandoned, Tracey's father shook his head.

'I know, love. No. Me and her mother have always said that if . . .'

But the woman wasn't listening. Before the fifth attempt she removed his cigarette to ensure that smoke would not appear in the picture when he began to speak.

'Right. Ready?'

He coughed and touched his tie, raising his hand to the onlookers who waved back before shushing each other into silence. The sound man held up his thumb.

'Mr Morton, it's been exactly a month since . . .'

This time, for better or worse, the half-minute interview was completed.

'How was it?' he asked, and the woman told him it was perfect, just perfect. She thanked him and shook his hand. He held it longer than was necessary. She said that he had been a great help and that she hoped everything worked out.

'See you in another month,' he said, stopping suddenly as he realised the implications of what he had said.

'Yes, well, perhaps we could come and interview you when Tracey returns home. Joyful reunions, and all that.'

As they left she gave him a card. This he held up for the small crowd to see.

The two cameramen loaded their equipment and waited impatiently. Twenty miles away a resident at an old folks' home had just touched a hundred and wanted to wave her telegram in front of the camera. It was already almost one o'clock and the old woman, convinced that her longevity was due to sea air and milk stout, had been sick and failing for the past six months. There was, therefore, some urgency.

Six o'clock news, tomorrow, the woman had said. Or the day after at the latest. He looked once again at the card she had given him and turned to face his home.

Behind the net curtains, her hand pressed against her cheek, stood his wife. She had refused to come out: her daughter's disappearance was still painful, too painful to perform for the cameras and lie about being hopeful and what a good girl she had been. Hair hung loosely down one side of her face, and there were dark rings around her eyes from crying and lack of sleep.

Devlin stood at the chalet window and watched the rain turn to sleet, pinking off the glass and collecting in strips along the narrow sill. Behind him his mother lay asleep, her tartan blanket folded over her feet and tucked beneath her arms into the sides of her chair. As usual, the smell of paraffin filled the room.

He watched the windows of the other chalets, some lit up, others dark and empty until the late spring when their owners would return to prepare them for the summer. The fragile fencing of one had blown down and the metal chimney stack of another had fallen into the garden, half buried now in the untidy grass like a spent rocket.

His mother coughed, smacking her lips as if expecting to taste something. Her head rolled back, her eyes still closed.

'You awake?' No answer.

From the recently ploughed field beside the chalets rose a flock of crows. Scared from their meal, they hung outstretched in the wind.

Devlin turned to look at the lighthouse and then back across the room to his mother.

'You awake?' he asked again, this time more softly.

Sitting at the table, he stared at her sleeping face, her moving lips and wet mouth. When she died he would move into the town, into his own flat; he would begin to live his life as he wanted to live it, to do the things she and the chalet prevented him from doing.

Ten years ago they had been going to pull down the chalets and re-house the permanent residents in council maisonettes. He had taken her to see them, but she hadn't wanted to leave, said the chalet was her home. There had been nothing he could say.

Eventually the council had reprieved the chalets, fearing that if they were demolished then the way would be clear for the extension of the caravan sites which were closing in from both sides. This had been at a time when the caravanning holiday-makers had been tolerated rather than encouraged, before their spending potential had been fully realised.

He watched her now and waited for her to say something in her sleep. Perhaps she was dreaming of when he had been a boy. Around him, the room grew dark, and in the darkness, the circle of blue flames between his knees, he thought about the girl and smiled at his own cleverness. Thinking of her, of the way she had struggled and what he had done, still excited him. He left his mother and passed through the bedroom to the cramped toilet, where he masturbated, standing and watching as the white liquid dripped, congealed and sank. The girl was there, and others. Veronica Priestley in her tunic, her stockinged legs, her hair, her face in his groin, begging him, pleading . . . And then there were only the white pearls against the porcelain bowl, the cold draught, his own irregular breathing, and his mother shouting his name, her voice rising in panic as she realised that she might be alone in the darkness.

'Says here that there's a report in a Bradford newspaper of a man claiming to have seen the missing girl. Says she's going by a different name and working in a launderette.' Morgan paused, continuing the article in silence. The headlines across the front page of the newspaper he held, his arms wide like a child's, announced 'Cub Scout Scandal' and 'Ex Call-Girl Claims "Charles Was Mine"'. There was a picture of the woman, a sincere look on her face and naked down to her thighs.

Norman looked up from his magazine. Sunday afternoons spent with the guests were one of the few things he truly disliked about owning a boarding house. Some Sundays he worked, others he spent in the garden or on his allotment, or walking with his binoculars along the abandoned railway line.

The pages of several newspapers lay spread around the room. On the sofa sat Derek and Veronica, tugging at the same page. Rita sat by the window, rubbing at a mark on her dress and inspecting her shoes.

Morgan sat in the chair beside the fire and continued to read out the headlines. He turned to look at the picture of the call-girl and licked his lips, pleased with the disgusted responses of Rita and Veronica, at Norman's glance towards the kitchen and Alice.

'Says that so far the local police have been unsuccessful in their attempts to trace the whereabouts of the girl, who was missing . . . "Unsuccessful in their attempts," it says here.' He lowered the page and stared at Norman, challenging him to respond.

Norman answered at once – calm, confident and policeman-like: 'Normal procedure. No point in raising people's hopes all the time. She'll turn up. She—'

'Already has done,' interrupted Morgan. 'In Bradford. Working in a launderette under a new name.'

'Not very likely, I wouldn't have thought. Not a fourteen-year-old schoolgirl with no money and no experience of living away from home.' Norman dropped the magazine to his lap and straightened his spectacles. He had, through his approach to the challenge, reversed the situation and gained the upper hand. He smiled at Derek who smiled back, nodding his head in agreement.

'You're likely to see a lot more reports of people claiming to have seen her, people all over the country I shouldn't wonder. People who—'

'Says here that in a statement given to Bradford police the man was able to positively identify the girl.'

'Ah, I see.' Norman allowed himself a further smile, took off his spectacles, wiped them and placed them carefully in their case, closing it with a loud click.

Veronica looked up. She had not been listening and was uncertain what the silence meant. Rita waved her hands and the room smelled of varnish.

Eventually, his hands clasped over his stomach and winking at Derek, Norman said: 'They'll have picked her up then, and brought her home, have they?'

Morgan read quickly to the end of the article. ' "It is not known at this stage whether the girl has been . . ." ' He stopped, sensing defeat.

From outside came the chimes of an ice-cream van, the same five notes, over and over.

Alice appeared in the doorway and asked if that was the ice-cream van she had heard. Derek said it was and stood up, offering to fetch some. Alice seemed undecided and turned back into the kitchen. Veronica told Derek to keep still – it was uncomfortable enough on the sofa without him moving about all the time. She pulled the sheet of paper from him, folding it into a manageable square.

Rita looked at the woman on the cover of Morgan's paper, at her neck and breasts, at her firm stomach and coloured nipples, ice-cubed to perfection. Morgan turned down the page to see what she was looking at. She shifted her gaze to his feet, jutting straight out from the seat, clear of the floor. Before he could say anything Norman got up, announced that he was going out for a breath of fresh air, and left the room. Anyone coming? Derek and Rita smiled back awkwardly, both reluctant to leave the warmth of the room. Morgan said nothing, and Veronica pointed out that anyone who wanted to go outside needed their head examining.

'Derek?' Norman waited in the doorway.

'Go on, get yourself out for ten minutes,' said Veronica, pushing him off the sofa. 'Give me a chance to get comfortable.'

As Derek stood up, she kicked off her slippers and lifted her legs, her skirt riding up to her knees. Alice reappeared in the doorway and asked them what they were up to. Weren't they going to stay and have a cup of tea? Going out? In this weather? Whatever for? Norman walked past her into the kitchen and Derek said 'A breath of fresh air', his tone suggesting that he would have preferred the tea.

'Oh, well. Don't let me stop you. Rain it said on the forecast. Rain and the possibility of wintry showers on higher land.'

'Right, then, we'll keep down off the mountains, Derek. No need for ropes or climbing boots.'

Derek laughed with him, cursed himself for being so weak and squeezed apologetically past Alice into the kitchen.

'You were saying about the kiddy who's gone missing. Poor

mite.' Alice was sitting in Norman's chair now, looking at Morgan and trying to ignore the naked woman with whom she was confronted.

'They think she might have turned up in Bradford,' Rita said. 'They think she's been seen. That's all.'

'Oh, well, I'm glad. Her mother must be sick with worry. Out of her mind with not knowing. Bradford. I've a sister used to live in Bradford. We used to visit.' Turning, she shouted into the kitchen. 'Bradford, Norman. Remember our Doreen?'

There was no answer, only the gentle click of a door closing.

'Men,' she said, and smiled at Rita, asking her the colour of her varnish. She watched Veronica's stockinged feet stretch towards her and said they'd been meaning to buy a new sofa for the past year or two, but what with the price of everything . . .

From above them came the sound of another door, and footsteps as Vincent crossed from the bathroom. Only Alice looked up.

Morgan read about the cub scout scandal, laughing to himself.

'I hope she is all right. The kiddy, I mean,' Alice said. 'It's a big place Bradford. Bigger than here.'

Only Rita took any notice of her, smiling and agreeing with what she said.

Veronica interrupted them to complain that the zip of a cushion had caught her tights, the third pair that week.

Morgan lowered his paper to look and Rita offered her varnish to stem the ladder. Alice said the kettle was about to boil and that what they all needed was a nice cup of tea. Could one of them close the curtains to keep the dark out? She left the room.

Rita and Veronica looked at each other and smiled, acknowledging the claustrophobic tedium of the afternoon and their helplessness to escape it.

December

I

Derek thrust the first blade through the box on a line with his wife's thighs, the second her breasts, the third from ear to ear through her head. He derived a certain pleasure from pushing in the swords, particularly the last. Between each thrust he paused long enough for the collective 'Oohs' and 'Aahs' to rise and fade. And as each shining silver tip slid into its corresponding slot, he whispered 'Take that!' Veronica usually either swore back at him or laughed derisively. 'Takes a bigger man than you,' she said this time, and in revenge Derek shook the upright box, knocking her around inside.

Before using the swords on his wife, Derek had demonstrated their cutting edge to the audience by holding up a carrot and slicing it cleanly in half. At the back of the theatre a small girl, mistaking the carrot for one of the rabbits seen earlier, screamed loudly. Veronica posed in the open box, one hand on her shoulder, the other on her hip, like an Eastern dancer. India, she supposed, or Egypt, China . . .

Devlin watched from the wings, and on the opposite side stood the troupe of six dancers, each of them making final adjustments to their costumes.

'The first sword goes in . . . *here!*' Derek slid it smoothly through the side of the box, while inside Veronica ensured that a corresponding point emerged at the opposite side. She judged the success of the operation by the audience's collective gasp and by the silent, waiting faces she could see through the slit between the box's two upper doors.

Seven years ago, for the first and last time in their marriage, Derek had been on the verge of leaving her. The attraction had been Molicia and her Performing Poodles (the two, or, more accurately, seven, being inseparable). They had met during Derek and Veronica's brief spell with a touring circus in the Midlands. Molicia – her real name, she insisted – had hand-sewn the name of each dog on its own jacket in gold thread.

Derek still had a photograph of Molicia. In it she looked younger than he remembered her – ten years younger, in fact.

She had given him the picture from a box containing several hundred others, all identical. In addition to her own leotarded figure were the six poodles, each one upright and with paws held out. She was looking at them and not the camera. It was, he remembered sourly, he who had insisted that she write 'To Derek, Love Molicia'. To which she had added the name of each dog. Derek did not like the dogs, one of which had bitten his ankle, and another walked upright across his exposed back during one of the affair's moments of real contact. The trailer was crowded with cups and trophies, photographs and paintings and other mementoes of the pampered animals upon which Molicia doted, and around which her life (professional and otherwise) revolved.

At their final meeting (although Derek had not realised it to be such at the time), she had insisted that the dogs line up and shake his hand as he left. It was for this that he had been prepared to abandon the rabbits, the doves, and Veronica. Molicia had made it very clear that dogs were the only animals she would ever consider working with. She had promised to write and confirm their plans, but since leaving the circus he had heard nothing.

Now all he had was the photograph.

Unwisely, Derek had informed Veronica prematurely of his plans to leave her, and consequently his hatred of Molicia and her poodles was sustained and prolonged by his wife's taunts.

'And the second sword – Quiet, please, we must have silence if the magic is to work – goes . . . here!'

He left the box and bowed to the audience, opening and closing his cape with impressive symmetry.

For her part, Veronica referred to their marriage as the Biggest Mistake of her Life, goading him with the names of other, often imaginary, men who might have married her and who might have made successes of straightforward, ordinary, anonymous jobs. She was not angry purely because of his brief relationship with Molicia, but because he had dared to plan ahead and to envisage a better future in which she played no part. Six years after their marriage she had had her own first affair with the manager of a night club at which they had secured a residency (largely, she afterwards boasted, as a result of her compliance). They said these things to hurt each other, but were always more successful at hurting themselves. Their marriage had become one of professional convenience – a contract from which neither was prepared to release the other whilst the chance of a Big Break or Golden Opportunity lay ahead. Veronica still waited for the Better Days Ahead, but only Derek still spoke of them.

'And the third sword . . .' This time there was a short but embarrassing delay and a clearly audible click before the silver point emerged.

'Stupid cow. Concentrate on what you're supposed to be doing.'

'Shut it!' She was peering through the gap at the dancers waiting to come on, and then at Devlin waiting to lower one of the curtains, behind which the box would be removed, followed by Derek and herself.

'And the fourth and final sword – my favourite,' he whispered, loud enough for her to hear, 'goes – right through her stupid head – *Here!*' He pushed the blade more forcefully than the others. The point appeared. Inside the cabinet, Veronica stubbed her toe and let out an involuntary cry of pain. For a second the audience remained silent. Devlin, thinking something had gone wrong, dropped the curtain before the end of the act. The dancers moved sideways onto the stage, and the girl who had screamed at the carrot screamed again.

Vincent walked the length of the Promenade. It was Alice's idea. It was she who said he would only get restless and frustrated sitting around the house all day. In the mornings he helped her with the housework and sometimes with the shopping. In the afternoons he left and walked towards the sea, following the same route each day to look out over the expanse of grey and white.

It had been raining earlier and the streets shone, threatened already with the prospect of ice later in the evening. His lips were cracked and painful; he licked them, feeling the hard skin and tasting the salt spray which coated his face. Yesterday he had applied for a job as Father Christmas, but had been passed over in favour of an older man who constantly rubbed his hands together, drank from a small bottle in his pocket, and told everyone concerned as loudly as possible how much he loved his grandchildren. Instead of references he brought photographs. He had lived in the town all his life. This, too, he seemed to think, would ensure his appointment – a month in the Fairy Grotto surrounded by fibre-glass walls and hollow fairies. Vincent's sense of defeat grew stronger.

He walked past the same café in which he had debated his future upon his arrival in the town.

The tide was in and the dirty waves broke in heavy swells against the sea wall, sometimes forcing a curtain of froth up and over the railings against which he stood. In the harbour the boats moved with the flow, spinning slowly on their mooring ropes and rising with the tide.

Passing the theatre, he paused to read the crowded names on the pantomime poster. Derek and Veronica were billed in thick black lettering in a curve across the top of the sheet. Mighty Morgan, Midget Man of Muscle, cast as the sorcerer's wicked assistant had his name printed in a line of slimmer lettering in the bottom corner. The show was billed to run until the end of December, after which the theatre closed for renovations until May, when the first of the summer engagements began.

In winter, the locals avoided the Promenade and sea which nourished the town in summer; they moved instead along the parallel streets of shops and bright displays, busying themselves with their preparations for Christmas.

Between these streets and the sea stood the deserted amusement arcades, their games and rides covered with dust sheets, standing like the ghosts of summer, a reminder and promise of what was to come.

Vincent pressed his face to the glass and studied the shapes and forms of the attractions. On the door was painted a juggling clown and the words 'Fun City'. Similar writing and motifs in moulded plastic adorned the brick supports of the interior. He remembered the arcades from his childhood holidays, and seeing them like this for the first time impressed upon him the difference between the seaside summers and winters. On warm weekends in October and March the arcades opened, testing the air and creating a market for their delights. But these were only half-hearted affairs, the last wring of a drying cloth.

As he peered through the glass, he saw a man cross the shadowed interior, heard him coughing. A light flickered and a siren sounded before being abruptly silenced. It was the sound heard from the depths of a ghost train on a warm day. Blue sparks fell from the roof and the dodgem cars began to twitch, shoaling together like fish and moving uncertainly around their wooden enclosure. The man walked amongst them, immobilising them one at a time, stepping from machine to machine,

74

kicking them apart. Soon they were all dead and no sparks fell. The light was extinguished and the man was gone.

In the winter some of the larger hotels stayed open to encourage conference trade, and for one weekend in January the town was filled with anglers, there for the sea-fishing competition. At night they lined the beaches with oil lamps, casting their coffin-shaped weights into the darkness. To the tips of their rods they attached bells which rang as the fish took the baits and were reeled in, disappointingly small and gasping for the sea on sheets of newspaper at the feet of the men who argued over their weight.

Now only a solitary angler stood against the harbour wall, stamping his feet and blowing against the cold, listening for his quivering bell with its promise of a fish. In the competition the lights stretched for as far as could be seen, three to four hundred sometimes.

In summer the Promenade was strung with colourful displays, hidden spotlights picking out the better hotels and the intricate patterns of the floral designs along the front. Not as impressive as Blackpool perhaps, but this was never the intention of the Tourist and Recreation Committee, whose hopeful plans for the town's future as a select family resort sagged with each new arcade and fast-food take-away.

That night, as they ate their tea, Norman told the assembled guests, Morgan in particular, that the search for the missing girl had been stepped down. Someone had reported an intruder in one of the chalets on the Happy Cliffs Caravan Camp, and it now seemed likely that the girl had spent the night there before leaving the town. According to information received, the chalet had been empty for six weeks but had been occupied on the night in question. Added to which – Norman paused for effect – a girl fitting the description of the missing girl had been seen hitching a lift three miles outside the town the next morning.

'Be in London by now,' said Derek, and Norman, angry at the suggestion (he being about to make the same unofficial guess), said that it was not his business to speculate.

Vincent, listening closely, said nothing and excused himself from the table.

Now it was Alice's turn to interrupt her husband, also with the suggestion that the girl would be many miles away. Everyone agreed and Norman, angry that she should align herself with

75

the others against him, informed them all that if the police worked on such unsubstantiated guesswork and rumour then they'd all be in a pretty mess. Only Derek agreed with him and Norman said, 'Thank you, Derek.'

As secretary of the local Guest House and Holiday Flats Association, Alice attended (during the closed season) weekly meetings where, more likely than not, she was called upon to be the chairperson for the duration of the discussion in which minutes were read and for which a xeroxed agenda was produced, often in time for the meeting itself.

During the summer, the women were too busy competing with each other to bother much with the aims of the association or its members' problems, but in winter it provided them with the opportunity to socialise and share their common problems.

The association had been formed five years previously to counter the Hoteliers and Restaurateurs Association – an altogether grander body with airs and pretensions well above the sweated labour in its steaming kitchens. At first the hoteliers had tried to prevent the Guest House Association being formed but, seeing it strengthen against their complaints, they had decided to look upon it as a harmless collection of housewife amateurs whose shared interests threw them together without the veneer of professionalism with which they, the hoteliers, cloaked themselves.

The hierarchical wheel was still turning, and it was now being debated whether or not the holiday-flat members ought to form an independent association of their own.

Being in the chair, it was Alice's responsibility to control the discussion and remain as objective as possible. But the meeting did not go well; Alice's mind was on other things.

Uncharacteristically, she had stopped to take stock of herself, to try and understand what it was that she found so unsettling. There was, she had half decided, more to life than this – living and dying with the seasons, hoping and despairing with the beginning and end of each summer.

Around her, the argument raged. The ladies, thirty in all (out of a membership of over three hundred), spread themselves around the living room of the Rothway Guest House, Proprietor J. Dixon, Mrs, ex-resident of Rotherham and magnet still to its steel mills and rolling shops. In one corner of the room was a bar, built in the shape of a bamboo hut with a thatched roof of plastic straw. It was backed by a poster of a tropical shore, hung with fairy lights and fronted by a row of pineapple-shaped ice buckets advertising drinks.

Mrs Dixon, her wrists fastened like an African tribeswoman's with bracelets and good luck charms, spoke out in favour of the guest-house owners. It was her home, her tea, her biscuits, and so few argued back. On the mantelpiece stood a line of black elephants, increasing in size from left to right. The remainder of the décor was colourfully standard for the guest houses which had sprung up throughout the residential areas like poppies (some said weeds) through corn, and which were still blossoming despite the pessimistic forecasts of those already in the trade.

Alice knew things had gone beyond her control when some of the self-catering exponents left in a group, demanding that a vote be taken throughout the entire membership. One woman spoke briefly about the problems she had encountered with a wholesale supplier of frozen fish, and the meeting was over.

More tea was served and those remaining gathered together to gossip about those who had left.

One of the women suggested to Alice that some of the members considered it – how could she put it? – slightly unusual for her to bother with the winter entertainment trade year after year. Surely it couldn't pay her to open her home for the month? Besides which, there was cheaper accommodation nearer the theatre. So why bother? And they were such strange people, the theatricals, so affected. Alice smiled but said nothing, leaving her accusers uncertain and forcing them to change the subject. They spoke instead of plastic floor covering to protect their carpets.

At three the rain stopped and the women dispersed.

Walking home, Alice began to think about what the woman had said. Was she simply jealous? She thought about Morgan and about Rita, and on a newspaper hoarding she saw the smiling face of the missing girl. The girl's disappearance upset her in a way she could not understand, and she studied the enlarged eyes and lips as though the face itself might contain the answer to what had happened.

Norman, in uniform, the shadow of his cap covering his eyes, stood with his hands on the shoulders of a thirteen-year-old boy and smiled as warmly as he could manage to the rest of the class and to the young woman teacher at their centre. The boy, who boasted of having a father in prison, grinned bravely for the benefit of his classmates. Norman fixed his smile – his Children's Friend smile – and resisted the urge to shake the boy until he cried. Where children were concerned, Norman had trouble controlling his real feelings: he disliked them, and he particularly disliked having to become a likeable policeman to coerce them into cooperating with him. The visit to the missing girl's school had been planned some time in advance but only Norman was free on the day of the visit. He handed round his cap and gloves for the younger children to try on and took along the handcuffs and obsolete truncheon for the older ones to wield.

A fat girl in a cardigan with horses knitted into it wanted to know where they kept the police horses; another asked the same about the dogs. Both said that they thought it was cruel to use animals, claiming rather wildly that hundreds got killed every year, shot and knocked down by lorries and things like that. The teacher said that she was sure they were mistaken, but the idea of all those animals getting killed appealed to the rest of the class and they took up the cause. Norman's grip on the boy's shoulders tightened. He felt the child flinch, a close-cropped head looking up, glimpsing a preview of his own future.

The cap and gloves, handcuffs and truncheon were handed back and the teacher announced the reason for Norman's visit. The children listened, thirty voices exploding with guesses about the whereabouts of their former classmate. The girl with the horses on her cardigan said that she would probably be a model or working in a hairdresser's in London or Leeds or somewhere like that. Or perhaps in a stables. That was what she wanted to do: work in a stables or a hairdresser's or . . .

'Now, did Tracey ever tell anyone that she might run away, or about a boyfriend perhaps?'

Thirty giggles of suppressed embarrassment. Norman had seen the marks on the necks of some of the girls in the class who can have been no older than the missing girl.

The teacher clapped them to silence and told them to stop being stupid; it was very serious, Tracey having gone off like that. The class subsided.

'Now, come on. Let's show Sergeant Protheroe how responsible we really are and let's stop wasting our time and his.'

'And that's a criminal offence – wasting police time,' Norman added, hoping to salvage something of the situation, a laugh perhaps. Instead, the children sat at their desks and stared at him resentfully. He began once again, asking for the names of those who had been close friends of Tracey. He asked them to think hard and not to be frightened of telling him anything they might know, anything that might help them to find her and bring her back home.

He knew that very little would come of the visit and that any significant clues to the girl's whereabouts would, after five weeks, have already come to light. The children repeated what they had seen and heard on the television, their imaginations rife with a wide variety of possibilities.

On the wall around the classroom were collages composed of magazine photographs and empty food packets. 'Very nice,' Norman said. The children turned to look around the walls, back to him and then to the teacher. He had fallen even further in their estimation and the boy with the father in prison asked him if he'd brought any slides. Norman saw only a criminal in the making. The class echoed the boy's question. The Road Safety Officer had brought slides of cars and road accident victims – although many of these they believed to be faked using actors and dummies.

It was the teacher who brought them once again to order. Norman waited, glancing at the clock and at his car parked in the corner of the yard. Already two small boys crouched beside it, studying the badge on the door. The woman saw him, smiled and told him not to worry. Norman smiled back, shook his head, and worried.

It was as he prepared to leave, the corridors filling with bells and running feet, that the prisoner's son voiced the opinion that the missing girl had been killed, murdered probably, and that that was why she was still missing. This raised a howl of disbelief from those who believed her to be working in a hairdresser's or as a model, and an even louder cheer from the boys, to whom the possibility of foul play and murder represented a much more exciting alternative. The teacher shouted for silence, but with little success as the various means and methods of murder were discussed.

Norman said, 'Yes, well . . .' and shook the teacher's hand. She smiled, apologising with her eyes, and said that she only wished she could have been more help. If the girl had come from a higher ability class, then perhaps . . . Norman told her not to worry and left unnoticed.

'Never thought of trying your hand at something else, something a bit more steady, settling down?' Norman held back the loose plank for Derek to climb through on to the path skirting the allotments. These walks had become a regular and, as far as Derek was concerned, unwelcome feature of Sunday afternoons.

'Steady?' Derek felt his trousers catch on a bramble. 'Steady? Oh . . . steady. Could have been an estate agent at one time. Probably have made a good job of it.'

'Estate agent. Mmmm. Good job, that.' Norman let the plank swing back into place.

'Could have gone in with my brother. Had the chance. But—' Derek threw up his hands. 'C'est la vie.' He smiled and shook his head reflectively to cover the lie.

'Show business, I suppose. Bright lights and all that? Glamour.'

Derek nodded. Ahead of him the path stretched into parallel lines of mud and water and wet grass. He wanted to turn back but Norman walked ahead, making comments on each allotment, describing their dormant crops and what they looked like in summer. Derek said only enough to include himself in the conversation, watching closely where he trod, swearing silently at the mud on his flared trousers, their stripe of red along the outer seam.

'. . . be a policeman. Lifelong ambition, you might say. People get the wrong idea. To listen to some of them talk, you'd think we—'

A man shouted and Norman shouted back. A dog appeared through a gap in the hedge, stopped, turned and stared at them.

The path turned to run alongside a railway embankment, spilled black clinker making the ground firmer.

'Oh, I can see the appeal of all that travelling around, new places, new faces and all that, but I've always been a home-bird myself.' Norman spoke in a tone which suggested that there was a norm to which everyone should adhere, an age by which they should be securely established and certain of their future. Derek was in no position to disagree. For one thing, he had lost his bearings and turned continually to search the gaps in the tall hedge for signs of the streets they had left behind.

'Good pension, reasonable working hours and overtime. Not to everybody's taste, mind. Not everyone would have the stomach for some of the things we have to put up with.'

'Oh? Such as?' said Derek, irritably, not really wanting to know.

Norman told him about the drowned body washed up at the height of last year's season and went on to recount several other incidents, stopping only to point out his own neatly arranged plot of land, bare except for its tripods of cane and upturned pots.

'See it in summer,' he said, and smiled at the memory. 'A sight for sore eyes, she is then. A sight for sore eyes.'

The two men stood side by side, one pointing, the other trying to appear interested. Starlings filled the hedge, waiting for them to leave. Scraps of paper blossomed white along the empty branches, and six yards from where they stood was the mound of rubbish beneath which the missing girl lay buried.

The circuitous path led them back on to the streets past an abandoned Methodist chapel, used now for the auction of clothing and fancy goods. On a cross beside it hung a wooden Jesus with graffiti sprayed across his chest. Norman stopped and shook his head, saying something about people having no respect. He raised his hand to a passing patrol car but received no reply.

Almost home, they passed a small enclosure in which a line of miserable-looking donkeys stood watching a bale of dirty hay. The ground around them had been trodden to mud, the crescent-shaped hollows full of water. Each animal wore a halter with a red leather flap over its forehead on which its name was written: names like Daisy and Dolly. The animals turned in unison to watch as the two men passed.

Derek felt wet and cold and miserable. In less than two hours he had a performance to give. And afterwards, Sunday would die fighting in a row with Veronica in their cramped dressing room. In an effort to cheer himself up he resumed what he had been saying about almost becoming an estate agent, adding lie to lie and smiling at the result.

Arriving home, Alice made a fuss and ushered them to the waiting table. Norman told everyone what an invigorating walk they'd had.

'Right, Derek?'

81

'Right.'

Veronica tugged at her husband's trousers, grimacing at the dried mud.

'Mud,' Derek said, looking to Norman for support, but receiving none.

2

Alice read an article in her magazine. In it a doctor, who had his own weekly TV series on which famous people talked about their illnesses and fears and fear of illness, was writing about the need to fantasise.

'*Fantasy and make-believe are as much a part of modern life as shopping and housework.*' Alice read on, a cup and saucer balanced on her knee.

'*Fantasy and make-believe, the retreat from so-called "reality" into a time and place where troubles vanish and where the cares and anxieties of modern day life are . . .*'

She stopped reading and thought about her own life.

'*We all need our dreams; we all fantasise about something – most of us without even realising it or without the courage to admit it to others!*'

She paused again, thinking hard for what her own fantasy might be.

Each time she looked down, the doctor's smile rose and fell like that of the Mona Lisa. She was disappointed in what he was promising; it was as though he had offered her something and then taken it away. Why couldn't he be more specific? Last week it had been breast cancer and women who led Completely Normal Lives.

The article unsettled Alice. '*Happy Dreams!*' it concluded. She looked again at the photograph and tried to guess the doctor's age, a task made difficult by his immaculate silver hair and the shadow which honed his chin and hid his neck. That something was lacking in her life, she was in little doubt; whether that something was her inability to fantasise (which she doubted), or to retreat from the routine of her existence (which she did not really understand), she was not so certain.

It was mid-afternoon, the only part of the day when she was alone in the house, and when she was most vulnerable to the sort of reflection prompted by the article. Perhaps she gave too much of her time and energy to others, made too many other lives easier at the expense of her own. What were women like herself supposed to fantasise about? Men? Themselves? What they might achieve if they were not what they were?

'Too much nervous energy,' Norman always said. 'Wear yourself out. Dead before you're fifty.' It was a cold joke, three years too late. Perhaps the article was aimed at a younger readership with its Successful Dinner Parties, Dressing On a Budget and Making the Most of Your Face. On the opposite page was an offer: three real butterflies, 'Colourful Inhabitants of the Exotic East, a Delight to Own and an Asset to Any Home, framed in glass on Real Hessian Backgrounds'. Alice looked at the creatures. Their bodies had been replaced with cork, only their elaborately shaped and coloured wings remaining, two wings probably not even belonging to the same insect. She studied the offer. £14.95 for three. How much did a butterfly cost?

In an hour her guests would return from the theatre. Derek and Veronica first, then Morgan, and then Rita. Vincent was still out looking for work.

The tea in Alice's hand had gone cold.

'Frankie Vaughan and the Woman behind Mr Moonlight.' Frankie Vaughan, a wide smile on his face, stood beside a blue-tiled swimming pool. Behind him was his home, its patio and perfect lawn, garden furniture, and a woman with golden hair and a tan to match her husband's. Alice read the article promising a meal for two for under a pound. She smiled to herself and then laughed. The sound of her laughter reassured her.

' *"Frankie and the woman behind Mr Moonlight."* ' She read the title aloud, repeating the words over and over, shouting them almost, laughing, and then, unaccountably, crying.

After a few minutes she stopped as suddenly as she had started, listening to the dying echo and looking at Frankie Vaughan's golden-haired wife, her polished nails, her smile, her jewellery. The paper wrinkled where a tear had fallen, the reverse print showing through.

Dare to dream? Why not? A Fascinating Addition to Any Home. Watch Your Friends' Reaction. A Friendly Butcher is a Must. It Needn't Cost the Earth. 'Too much nervous energy,' Norman said. 'Dead by the time you're fifty.' Dead.

Derek wore a white nylon, polo-necked shirt beneath a navy

84

barathea blazer, the breast pocket of which was embroidered in gold and scarlet thread. 'Latin,' he explained when anyone bothered to read the inscription. If they wanted a translation he made one up. For special occasions he wore a tan-coloured paisley-patterned cravat, tucking it inside his summer open-necked shirts or letting it hang loose over his chest, as now. Veronica told him that the cravat was ridiculous and made him look effeminate. He told her that she didn't know what she was talking about, but later stared at himself in the mirror, wondering. The blazer he had bought second-hand.

She, he retaliated, wore too much make-up, and wore it badly, like her clothes and hair. But Veronica was largely impervious to this kind of criticism, drawing eyebrows and lips where none existed and dabbing a rosy outdoor glow either side of her nose after a morning in bed. The clothes she wore hugged her figure (hugged was the word she preferred; clung sounded a little too desperate) and, in its turn, her figure expanded to take advantage of any space or weakness in the cheap skirts or blouses she continued to buy. Her problem was not that she was particularly fat, but that she thought herself thinner. Likewise with her age. Recently she had taken to wearing tights with glitter woven into them.

Had they been strangers, Derek and Veronica would have found the other an attractive proposition. Familiarity and contempt had worn them down. They sat at either ends of the sofa, the remainder of the household coughing and shifting uncomfortably around them.

'And how about you, Mister Morgan?' Alice asked, folding her reading glasses into their case and patting the magazine on her lap. Everyone in the room looked up, first at Alice and then at Morgan. The question meant nothing; it was simply Alice's way of breaking the long silence.

'And how about me what, exactly?' Morgan crashed his hands into the paper and stared directly at Alice, his lips alternating between a smile and a scowl. Alice did not know what to say. Her hand moved to her throat in a nervous, defensive gesture. Norman looked at his wife and then at Morgan.

Rita looked at Vincent, and Vincent nodded, as though they were vague acquaintants passing on a busy street.

'I er . . . the girl, she means,' Norman said.

Alice nodded, still plucking at the skin of her neck. Why was the man so unnecessarily rude?

'What girl?' Morgan knew precisely what girl.

'Oh, for— the missing girl, that's who.' Derek slammed his own paper down. He was wedged between Veronica and Rita, his comparatively thin legs pressed into the low sofa.

'Oh, *that* girl! You want to know what I think, do you?' Alice nodded.

'Why? Suspect me, do you?'

'No, Mr Morgan, I–I only . . .'

'It's all right, love.' Norman put his arm on his wife's sleeve to reassure her.

Through the wall came the sound of someone shouting and a child crying.

'Thin walls,' Vincent said, knowing it was the wrong thing to have said even before the words were out. The crying continued. Everyone listened.

'Not really,' Norman said.

'No, not thin exactly,' Vincent began, 'more . . .' He turned to Rita and smiled. She smiled back. 'Yes, well . . .'

Norman made a snorting sound and picked up the magazine he'd been reading. On the cover were pictured a dinosaur, a double-decker bus and a naked man. He read aloud their respective weights and life-expectancies.

Silence returned, during which the shouting through the walls resumed, individual words being clearly audible. At each shout Alice looked to the clock, as though the timing of each outburst was of some significance.

'And it's Mighty not Mister.' The paper tightened in expectation of the replies.

'What? Sorry. Pardon?'

'I said it's Mighty not Mister. Mighty Morgan not Mister Morgan.'

The distinction would have been abandoned there had not Veronica said: 'What! All four foot ten?' and laughed.

Rita and Vincent smiled neutral smiles, unsure whether or not to endorse what was happening.

The paper tightened further.

These were the kinds of loose ends Veronica pounced upon and drew as tight as cheese-wire. 'Mighty Mouth more like!' She continued laughing.

'Veronica, I don't think—' Alice touched the sofa.

'Well. Who does he think he is? "Mighty Morgan." What's so

86

f—flippin' mighty about him that makes him so bloody special? Arrogant little b—'

'Language, please.' Norman touched Alice, thus forming a chain towards the sofa and Veronica.

'Well, the jumped-up little . . .' The initial, irresistible gibe was pulling at something deeper; it was something all of them felt towards Morgan, however inadmissible, but which only Veronica was likely to put into words. And because they all felt it none of them said anything in Morgan's defence, preferring instead to listen to what she had to say and then react. It was through other people's uncertainty and cowardice that Morgan won, or appeared to win, his arguments.

Behind his paper he sensed the swing of opinion against Veronica because of the language she was using and because of the faint line she had crossed towards vindictiveness.

'Four o'clock,' Alice said.

Norman said, 'Yes.'

'As late as that?' Vincent added, clapping his hands on to his knees.

Rita nodded and looked outside.

Only Derek and Veronica, united in their hatred for the midget, maintained their staring vigil, guessing at his true reactions behind the open sheets.

'Says here that a man chopped his wife's body into tiny cubes and got rid of her a bit at a time in the dustbin.' The voice was followed by a wheeze of laughter.

It was a crime confessed, and so Norman moved in to take his place in the discussion. To begin with he stroked his chin and nodded.

'Says it took him three months and she weighed eight stone.'

Norman pursed his lips, as though making a private calculation.

'By that reckoning,' Morgan went on, 'you'd need from now until the year after next, Derek.'

'Bastard.' The word was whispered and no one heard. Veronica dug her nails into the palm of her hand.

Alice wanted to say that perhaps enough had been said. She wanted, specifically, to say it to Morgan, but the word 'Mighty' seemed somehow ridiculous, something she could not bring herself to say.

*

Roland Trotter arrived at his garage to find the doors already open and someone standing beside his Jaguar.

'Devlin?'

'Missed the bus.' Devlin stepped out into the light.

'A lift? Yes, of course. But the doors . . . how . . .?'

'Easy. I can open anything.'

As Roland approached the car Devlin climbed into the passenger seat, having somehow managed to open that door too, and sat smirking as he waited for Roland to join him.

'I saw it going, but by the time the daft old cow had done the breakfasts—'

'Breakfasts?'

'The bus. That's why I was late.'

'Oh, I see.' That Devlin had offered an explanation without being asked made Roland uneasy. He watched him now fiddling with the heat controls.

'Your mother all right, is she?'

'Much the same.'

Roland turned the car towards the front of the house. His wife and oldest daughter, Andrina, were standing at the window.

'I have to drop my daughter off at school.'

'I know.'

Roland pressed the horn and his wife and Andrina came to the doorway. The girl complained that Devlin was in her seat and stood with her arms folded across her fat chest, made even fatter by her coat and scarves.

'Kids,' Roland said, too softly for his wife to hear, and hoping Devlin might take the hint. But he did not, and after half a minute of stand-off Andrina climbed into the back seat.

'This is Mr Devlin, love. We're giving him a lift. He missed his—'

'I know who it is.'

He hoped she would say no more, that she wouldn't repeat anything she might have overheard him say about the man. She caught his worried glance in the rear-view mirror and smiled.

'Did your mother give you anything for sweets, petal?' He knew that she had. Andrina smiled and shook her head.

As they waited to enter the flow of traffic, Roland saw Devlin watching his daughter in the mirror. She was returning the glances as though the two of them shared a secret, the disclosure of which would injure him alone. That, he told himself, was ridiculous.

'He's smoking,' the girl announced as Devlin lit a second cigarette.

'Try and sit still, Andrina, I can't quite see out of the back window.'

Devlin half turned to face the girl. 'How old are you, then?'

'She's fourteen.'

'Nearly fifteen.' She made it sound like twenty-five. She smiled at Devlin, and Devlin winked back.

'She likes horses, don't you, petal? Stuff like that,' Roland said in an attempt to change the subject.

His daughter scowled at him. 'He's always called me petal since I was little.' She leaned forward in her seat, inhaling the smoke. She made the word sound obscene.

'But you're a big girl now, eh?'

She smiled and pushed out her hidden chest, causing her chins to concertina together.

'Fat,' thought Roland. 'Does he mean fat?'

'And I bet she has all the boys chasing after her . . .'

'Well, actually, she's too interested in horses and riding to, er, have much time for . . . That right, pet— love?'

She scowled at him again, and taking a small mirror from her bag, studied her face, making kissing motions and glancing at Devlin to ensure he was still watching.

They arrived at the school and Roland manoeuvred into the line of cars from which other children were beginning to emerge.

'What is it today, love? History, arithmetic . . .?'

She looked at her father as though he was an embarrassing younger brother.

'I bet she likes stuff like PE and dancing,' Devlin said.

Andrina smiled, as if to agree with him, and climbed clumsily out. She straightened her coat and, as her father bent to kiss her, walked away.

'Must cost a few bob to keep her at a school like that,' said Devlin.

Roland didn't answer; he was concentrating on getting back out into the traffic. Fat. Had he meant fat? 'Must be a bit cold out in the chalets this time of year,' he said eventually, realising that everything he had said so far had amounted to either an apology or an admission of weakness.

'Yeh. Bit cold. We sometimes get kids on horses riding through the camps. She got a horse, then?'

'Not yet. Not one of her own.'

'They come out over the lighthouse field. All ages. Small, right up to eighteen, nineteen.'

After that they continued their journey to the theatre in silence.

Roland parked at the centre of the empty car park and, pointing, suggested that something be done about the abandoned rides and discarded props which lined one wall. Devlin nodded and walked away in the opposite direction. Locking the car, Roland tested the handle in an attempt to understand how it had been opened.

'You can come in the front with me,' he shouted. But Devlin simply raised his arm and continued towards the rear entrance. 'Ungrateful—' thought Roland, and walked briskly to his own office, where he would smoke his morning cigar and wait until something turned up for him to do. He would hear Devlin moving around the empty building, but would, as most days, avoid him for as long as possible. *Nearly fifteen* and after that *nearly sixteen* and after that . . .

The theatre was cold, and as he unlocked the cashiers' booths, Roland heard Devlin whistling. He walked from the foyer to the auditorium, but saw nothing. The room smelled damp and unused, and this, rather than being filled with shouting, applauding people, had always seemed to Roland to be its natural state. Each morning, especially in winter, it was difficult for him to dispel the idea that the theatre hadn't been abandoned and empty for the past ten years.

Major Halifax arrived a fortnight after Norman's suggestion that he should be invited to visit Vincent. Only Norman looked forward to the visit, and of the three only he genuinely believed that any good would come of it.

Major Halifax had some difficulty in finding the house and parking his car. He smoked his pipe as he counted along the colourful windows, trying to understand his own motives for making the call and seeing someone who was probably already beyond any help the Friends might have been able or willing to offer. It was the first time that the Society had been called upon in this capacity and he was not sure what was expected of him, preferring to judge the man without seeing him. He would much rather have discussed Vincent's case in the Council chambers with the remainder of the executive body of the Friends, including one Lord and one Lady (both senile octogenarians), where at least his opinions would have been shared ('Hear hear') and where any plan of action would have been deferred by popular disinterest. The wives and children of prisoners were the closest the Friends had previously come to the penal system.

In the living room, Norman and Vincent waited. Norman wore the polished shoes and matching shirt and tie which announced him as a policeman even on the few occasions he pretended otherwise. Vincent, at Norman's insistence, wore a borrowed suit and a tie with a yellow motif whose origin they could only guess at.

The major arrived, and Vincent overheard Norman's obsequious welcome. The man entered the room and looked at Vincent as he might look at a child awaiting punishment.

'Vincent, this is Major Halifax, chairman of—'

'Retired, I'm afraid.'

'What?'

'Major. Retired.' He repeated the word twice, making it quite clear that he still considered himself as Major and that that was how they should address him.

'Yes, of course. Major Halifax, retired. Also a member of the Town Council, Civic Society, Rotary, er . . .'

'Masons. Treasurer.' The Major smiled and looked to one side, as though it had not been he who had offered the information.

'And a good many other local charities and good causes,' Norman concluded.

'Very nice,' Vincent said, wondering whether to offer his hand or bow slightly.

Norman continued speaking and the Major looked around the cramped room, pretending to admire the décor.

'This is Vincent,' Norman said eventually. 'My wife's brother.' ('My brother-in-law' would have taken too great an effort.)

'Ah, yes, er, Vincent.' The Major held out a hand, speaking loudly and smiling broadly as if he had just noticed the man at a civic reception or handed him a trophy.

'Thank you,' Vincent said, meaning to add 'for coming', but

91

being interrupted by Norman who told the Major that he had told Vincent all about the good work done by the Friends.

'Yes, well, we . . . er, do our . . . er, best.' The Major spoke slowly, pausing between each word as though he was having to think of the next. He was only really happy when shouting orders to his wife and domestic help in the privacy of his own home. And even then they laughed behind his back. Sometimes his wife saluted.

Norman said he was being too modest, and stood between the two men making uncertain movements with his hands, half translator, half probation officer.

'The Major commanded a tank corps in Africa and Italy, right?'

'Only during the war.' It was meant as a joke but no one laughed.

'It was largely as a result of his efforts that the Friends were formed.'

The Major made a modest gesture with his hand that suggested he should go on.

Vincent smelled the stale tobacco which impregnated the man's clothes and breath.

Ignoring Vincent, the Major asked Norman how his commanding officer was keeping, referring to the man by his first name. He then touched the bowl of the pipe which protruded from his pocket. Norman immediately left the room to find an ashtray.

'Filthy . . . habit . . .' he said to Vincent between sucks. 'But it's been almost fifty years now . . . and it's done me . . . no harm yet.'

'No. Right.' Vincent ran his finger down his tie, and the Major brushed his moustache with his forefinger.

Norman returned next with a tray of tea, insisting that they carry on and not let him interrupt them.

The Major resumed his history of the Friends while, beside him, Norman nodded and repeated key words. Vincent interjected with an occasional question.

The Major now told an anecdote about an Indian whose brother had been hung in connection with something to do with a buffalo. Vincent wondered at the connection.

'The Major served in India,' Norman said.

'No, actually . . . I, er . . . I never did. Shame, really, but there you go. Left the poor blighter strung up for ten days. Stiff as leather when they cut him down.' The porcelain tiger on the mantelpiece reminded the Major of another story, but because his absence from India had been exposed, he declined to tell it, returning instead to his outline of the aims of the Friends.

The whole occasion reminded Vincent of his trial: he felt trapped, overtaken by events and people who hardly knew him.

'We can't, er . . . can't make any promises, but I'm almost certain that—'

But Vincent had had enough. 'Any more tea in the pot, Norm?' And once the words were out he took great comfort from them.

The Major stopped in mid-sentence, looked at Vincent and then turned to stare at Norman. Didn't the man want to be helped?

Norman was embarrassed and confused. 'Yes, er no. I er . . . Another cup, Major?'

What were they up to? Was it a conspiracy? The Major sucked hard on his cold pipe, the skein of blood vessels draped over his cheeks and nose turning blue with the effort.

It was then that the front door slammed and a woman in an imitation leopard-skin coat came in accompanied by what appeared to be a child, but turned out to be a midget. Was he seeing things? He looked towards Norman, but Norman was busy collecting the cups.

'Who's your friend? What's the suit for? Somebody's funeral?' The midget was laughing. Not only that, but it was climbing on to the sofa to sit beside him! The woman sat opposite, massaging her feet and complaining at the crowds. What was happening?

'This is, er, Major Halifax,' Vincent said, loosening his tie. 'He's a founder of the Friendly Police Society or something. He's a friend of Norm's.'

'Oh, Army man, then.' Rita smiled. 'Uniform and all that.'

'Any medals?' The midget sat forward to stare over his stomach.

'Actually, I er . . . I er . . .'

Vincent helped the Major out by announcing that Norman was preparing another pot of tea, adding that it, too, probably came from India. India or China or wherever.

Rita took off her coat, revealing stockinged legs. The midget whistled like a hooligan at the cinema.

In the kitchen, Norman gripped the edge of the sink and stared into the empty plastic bowl. 'No,' he said quietly, over and over.

Behind him he heard Vincent ask the Major for a light and Morgan ask him how many men he had killed. He heard the Major splutter like a drowning man. And then the kettle began to whistle, shutting out every other sound and blowing steam into his face.

In Danes Head village, in the small bar of the Lobster Pot, the old men, surrounded in summer by their haul of tourists, traded in their half-truths about the past in exchange for drinks. Mostly they spoke about what was expected of them – the sea and the time when their relationship with it had been far more delicate and uncertain.

Now, in winter, it seemed as if the present did not exist and that they lived purely on past events in which the truth had long been submerged in the elaborate manner of its telling. Often the momentum of their summer lying carried them through into the winter. Some nights they said nothing at all, but sat silently with the landlord, the clock clucking and the sound of their ivory dominoes filling the bar.

On his nights off, and when the theatre was closed, Devlin spent his time in the bar with these old men. The younger farm workers and those who found seasonal work in the town's amusement arcades or with fishing parties congregated in the other bar. In summer they sat beneath coloured umbrellas in their black leathers and denim, their helmets on their knees, their bikes tethered to the cobble wall behind them. But Devlin felt more comfortable with the old men.

On the walls of the bar, and on those of the summer-only room in which basket meals were served, were modern sepia-toned prints of masted ships run aground, of copper-faced women beside wicker baskets piled with silver bodies, or on cobbled runways with their bearded husbands, fish spread across the ground at their feet. Only one of the prints was of a local scene. It didn't matter that the others were of Whitby or the south coast or packet barges sailing up the Thames. It was the sea that mattered, the drowning, profitable sea.

In summer the tourists ducked their heads and came into the small room, remarking on its stained and faded décor as they might point at a set piece in a museum. On one wall hung a lobster pot, stained brown and disintegrating with age and constant inspection. It had been bought and installed by the brewery, made especially for wall-hanging.

The distance between the chalet and the village was almost two miles, half an hour at a running walk. Devlin arrived and made something of his arrival by asking if anyone wanted a drink and clapping his hands noisily against the cold. Into a room full of old men he had escaped from a room full of an old woman playing out her role of mother with her painful movements and useless memories. Night after night of inane conversations about the television programmes she had watched, about how she felt, what she had done . . . The old men at least were content to make no demands of him other than that he became one of them as they sat out the winter with their backs to the sea.

Only with the landlord did he have any real conversation. They discussed the village, the town, the coming season, Christmas . . . They discussed the missing girl and the landlord said he wouldn't be surprised if she turned up murdered, washed up by the sea somewhere. 'A bad do all round,' he called it, no real feeling in his voice. Devlin countered by saying that thousands of young girls ran away every year and that if he had the money or the freedom he'd be off himself. The barman nodded: anyone who had the means and inclination left the village to live and work in the town, some went even further – to Leeds or Sheffield or Rotherham, returning most summers to sow the seeds of discontent amongst those who remained behind to watch the village die amidst a flurry of holiday-home buying, double glazing and stone-effect cladding.

Devlin derived a perverse pleasure from talking about the girl, convinced that his ability to do this was proof that his crime would remain undetected.

The landlord produced a newspaper in which a short report said that the local police were continuing their enquiries but that they thought the girl had already left the area.

'Well-known fact that if they don't come up with anything in the first few days, then they're never likely to come up with anything,' Devlin said smugly.

The landlord said he supposed he was right, and refilled his glass without being asked. Devlin leaned back against the bar, drank his third drink quickly, and smiled to himself at the confession already loosening inside his head.

3

Norman, Vincent and Morgan sat together in the living room. Norman and Vincent on the sofa, Norman reading one of his wildlife books, Vincent studying his finger and repeatedly humming the same few bars of a tune none of them recognised. Morgan sat opposite them in the room's only comfortable chair – Norman's chair – his feet swinging free of the ground. He too was whistling, and watching the reflection of his swinging legs in the burnished brass plate of the unlit gas fire.

It was late morning and the room was filled with bright winter sunlight, penetrated only by the sounds of traffic, birds and distant barking dogs.

Earlier, Alice and Rita had been with the men, but had left together to inspect the town's weekly market, leaving the three men to drown in the awkward silence which rushed in to fill the room as the door closed behind them.

Vincent envied Morgan his separate chair, hardly daring to move in case he disturbed Norman. Morgan wrapped his stubby fingers round his knee and read aloud the title of Norman's book. It was the beginning of a discussion and the whistling stopped.

'You go in for all that stuff, then? Animals, rivers, Wonders of the World, that sort of junk?'

'Hardly junk,' Norman said, looking up and pressing the large book to his chest protectively. 'It's all a question of self-improvement. Right, Vincent?'

Caught unawares, Vincent echoed, 'Self-improvement,' and nodded uncertainly.

'Junk,' Morgan repeated.

Norman smiled tolerantly and tutted. 'Inter-force General Knowledge starting up again in March,' he said to Vincent. 'Got to get myself up to scratch. Gen up on a few points.'

Vincent said, 'Yes, I suppose so.'

' "Gen up on a few points," ' Morgan mimicked. 'It's junk. Crap.'

Vincent winced, caught in the crossfire.

'I've a book on coral reefs yet to get through. Great Barrier Reef, that sort of thing. South Seas. Indian Ocean.' He spoke facing Vincent. The Major Halifax episode had been quickly forgotten.

Morgan shifted forward and pointed to the book in Norman's lap. 'Go on, then. What's in there that you didn't already know?'

'What's in there? What's in there?' Norman was shouting with mock-incredulity and looking at Vincent as though expecting him to join in the chorus. He laughed as he rapped his knuckles on the cover of the book. 'Books are knowledge and knowledge is power. There's many a famous man come to that conclusion before now.' He turned smugly to Vincent and the two men nodded. It was only in situations such as this that Norman would accept that he and his brother-in-law had anything in common: it was a bond forged weakly in opposing a third party (as were most of the relationships in the claustrophobic household).

Silence followed in which Morgan whistled the first few notes of his tune. Another nod from Norman, victory assumed.

Then Morgan spoke, his timing immaculate: 'Probably, but I doubt if they had bumper colour books of wildlife in mind when they said it. Or that they ordered them cut-price from a book club.'

Vincent wanted to smile.

Morgan did.

'Nothing wrong with book clubs. It's—'

'I had a book like that once,' Morgan interrupted, his smile spreading.

'Oh?'

'Yeh. Coloured it all in with wax crayons.'

Now Vincent wanted to laugh. The bond between him and his brother-in-law was not so strong as Norman would have liked to believe.

'I hardly think so. Not at . . . at . . . .' Norman looked inside the book. 'Not at £12.95. Not at that price you didn't. Brand new, this book.' He held it up for them to see, careful to let neither of them touch it. Nor did he mention that he had paid only 99p for it as an introductory offer.

'Go on, then, amaze us,' Morgan said.

'You think it's as simple as that, do you? Listen, the world of wildlife – Nature – is so full of amazing facts and figures that I doubt any one man could learn it all in a lifetime. There are so many scarcely believable things that—'

'Such as?'

'Such as! Such as!' Repetition plus emphasis was one of the techniques employed by Norman to undermine his opponent. Other than with new recruits to the Force, it was seldom as effective as he liked to think.

'Such as?' Morgan remained calm.

'Such as the starfish,' Norman said, the book falling open at the picture of a starfish and no other scarcely believable wonder of nature coming readily to mind.

'The starfish?' Vincent said.

'Yes. The starfish.' Norman replied, exasperated that they had joined forces against him, and that he had chosen that particular, not very remarkable animal to try and prove his point. He was committed now to explain what was so wonderful about the starfish when he would rather have discussed, say, snow leopards or okapi.

Morgan, realising Norman's error, became more insistent: 'Yes, the starfish. What about it?'

'It! It!' The trick was failing. 'There's more than one, you know. You make it sound as if there was only one. Seldom the case in nature, seldom the case.' He turned to Vincent with a confident nod which was not returned.

'Only one giraffe, only one polar bear,' Morgan said, taking advantage of Norman's confusion and the fact that the book had fallen shut.

'The starfish family . . .' Norman began, assuming his officer-at-the-desk, friend-in-the-public-eye voice and searching desperately back through the book. 'The starfish . . . ah, yes.' He read out the Latin name. Family. Species. Genus. The words impressed him; Latin always did: it gave even the most ordinary animal (or fish) some kind of importance. 'The starfish, you might be interested to hear—'

'Not really.'

'—is capable of rapid processes of regeneration and—'

'Fancy!'

'—is able to grow entire new limbs from a remaining stump in a matter of weeks, sometimes days.'

'Why?' The question came from Vincent.

'Why what?'

'Why does it need to grow new arms? How does it lose its old ones?'

'I hardly think it's as simple as that, Vincent. They get attacked, eaten. Predators, sharks . . .' Having strayed from the text, he was stumbling for the explanation. 'The, er, this amazing power is the starfish's defence mechanism against the hordes of predators which abound around all coastlines, all of which search out the humble starfish in search of an easy meal. In some of the warmer oceans—'

'Deserves all it gets, then,' Morgan said. 'What kind of a bloody stupid trick is that? Stands to reason that if it doesn't matter whether it loses a leg or not—'

'Limb,' interrupted Norman.

'Leg, limb, whatever. It stands to reason that if it doesn't matter to it to lose one, then whatever wants to eat one isn't going to bother too much about pulling one off. It seems to me like it's just setting itself up to get pulled to pieces.'

'Like worms,' added Vincent, smiling weakly as both men turned to face him, confident that his contribution was a positive one. 'If you chop a worm in half, both halves become new worms. So you can chop as many, er . . . chop them in half and, er . . .' His explanation petered out.

Norman knew this to be true, or at least he had heard it often enough to believe it to be true. After all, he was the allotment owner; if anybody should know about things like that, then he should. 'Ah, yes, similar powers of, er . . . of . . .' – his finger ran down the page – 'of regeneration. Very similar. Same principle. Vastly different in practice, of course. Different species and everything.' He spoke with an air of authority which did nothing to disguise his ignorance. He was searching desperately for another Latin name with which to impress them.

'Natural victims,' Morgan said, and Vincent nodded. Norman wished he had thought of the term himself. (He remembered later about the starfishes' ability to push their stomachs out through their mouths and envelop their prey, coating it in gastric juices to decompose it before eating it. But this came too late and only added to his sense of defeat.)

'Alice and Rita back soon, I shouldn't wonder,' he said, checking his watch with the clock on the wall.

'Like lizards' tails,' Vincent said suddenly. 'They can grow new tails if one gets pulled off. I've seen it on the telly. Complete new tails. Go on, Norm, look in your book. See what it says about lizards.'

Norman's grip on the book tightened. The conversation had left him behind. And he was the expert on animals. It was his book and he would look up what he wanted. He winced also at the use of the familiar name. The men at the station used it every day, but even after thirty years it still irritated him.

'And puffer fish,' Morgan shouted. 'You can see 'em in gift shops. All dried and spiky and blowed up for two pounds for a dried fish. And whatsits, horse-fish, or whatever you call 'em.'

'Horse-fish,' Norman repeated, trying to remember what a horse-fish looked like or what he knew about them.

'I think he means sea-horses,' Vincent said.

'Of course he does,' Norman said quickly, suggesting by his tone that it was what he had understood him to mean all along. He was now trying desperately to remember something about sea-horses with which to impress them.

'That's it – sea-horses. You can buy dried sea-horses as key rings for ten bob. Had one once. Broke.' Morgan paused to remember his broken sea-horse key ring.

'I hardly see the connection,' Norman said, eager to return to the discussion and steer it towards something he knew about.

'No, but it's right what he says, Norm. Some animals are, like, natural victims, setting themselves up to be taken advantage of. You don't get people buying dried mackerel key rings, or stuff like that, do you? He's right: some animals make things too easy.'

'Like ostrich feathers,' Morgan interjected.

'And pheasants,' added Vincent. 'See, if they didn't have such colourful feathers they—'

'Plumage,' corrected Norman.

'Such colourful plumage, then they wouldn't get people knocking them off just to stick in their hats, would they? Stands to reason.'

Norman nodded to himself, remembering the four swans he had seen the previous summer on the boating pond island, brilliantly white with orange beaks and black faces, feathers the length of his arm, all with their delicate necks broken, their breasts bloodied with air-rifle pellets where they had been repeatedly shot. He remembered also the attendant behind him, crying, the massive nests and the helplessly cold eggs.

Morgan was saying something to Vincent, and Norman felt a sudden resentment against both men. To them it was just a joke. When had they last read a book or had to collect four dead swans in a sack and bury them?

'Shut up,' he shouted, realising too late that they had already stopped talking. 'Sorry,' he added, rubbing his forehead. 'Bit of a headache. Too many split shifts.' He hated himself for the apology.

Morgan, considering the argument won, clapped like a child.

'Can't think what's keeping Alice,' Norman said, ignoring him, crossing the room to replace his book, staring through the net curtains at the traffic and people outside. 'Feels funny being at home in the mornings; I've not been on afternoons for nearly two months.' He stood with his back to the men, an awkward stranger in his own home, lost without his wife.

Veronica strained to hear what Derek was saying. She heard laughter, the scrape of a chair and then his voice. She heard Roland Trotter, calling him Mr Priestley, but then nothing more. Derek was there in an attempt to renegotiate the terms of their contract. The pantomime had been a greater success than expected and would very likely run through to the middle of January. The other performers would all in turn make the same approach, demanding an increase in their pay for the additional fortnight.

As she waited, she read the Forthcoming Attractions notice-board, still with its previous summer's itinerary of the names and faces who came and went, who drew the crowds, and who took more money for a single night's performance than she and Derek would earn between them in a week. Morgan was also in the theatre, supplementing his wages by helping Devlin to clear a storeroom in preparation for its conversion into a dressing room.

Vince Hill. Youth Orchestra. International Singing Star. As seen on The Two Ronnies. One Night Only. A Night Out for the Ladies. Beside each name smiled a photograph, oval and wreathed, younger and more vital than the performers themselves. She studied the faces, imagining her own there, envy getting the better of contempt. She watched other magicians and their shapely assistants rise to stardom on the television. With each one that rose she felt herself even deeper in the anonymous pool in which she and Derek still struggled. Once, at a concert in

Batley, they had shared a dressing room with Paul Daniels, and this – for Veronica at least – made their comparative lack of success and attendant benefits even harder to bear. Her sense of failure made her bitter, leaving her with a feeling of such helplessness that she preferred not to think about it. Sometimes she tried to convince herself that it was Derek who prevented them from moving up, who kept them where they were. But this, too, she did not really believe. 'Treading water,' he called it, adding that it was more than most entertainers could manage these days. 'Drowning,' she called it, and clutched at whatever might rescue her.

As she stood in the hallway studying the poster, Devlin crept up behind her. He jabbed her waist with both hands, stepping quickly back to avoid her blow.

'You stupid bastard!' She pushed him along the corridor, telling him to keep his voice down, that the manager and her husband were discussing business.

Devlin forced a loud laugh and said that he didn't care. Leaning diagonally across the corridor he offered her a cigarette which she accepted before suggesting that he got on with whatever it was he was supposed to be doing – mucking out the rabbits or something. He smiled and wiped his mouth with the back of his hand, waiting for her to finish.

'He doesn't scare me, you know, Mister high and bloody mighty Trotter.'

She told him to keep his voice down or he'd be overheard. She looked over his shoulder at the closed door.

'So?' he asked, even louder. 'You want to get rid of him. He's hopeless. Ten a fuckin' penny, magicians, these days. You should see the agents' sheets we get in here. Nine out of ten are magicians.'

She wanted to argue with him, to ask him how it was that she and Derek still managed to make a living at it. But instead she turned away, not wanting to hear what he might tell her. She blew smoke towards him. He watched it break and curl around his head.

'You want to get yourself a proper husband with a decent job, something steady.'

'Like you, you mean – odd-job tea boy?'

Devlin clenched his fist, knowing that a denial would only spur her on.

'Stage manager,' he said and turned away down the corridor. Veronica followed him and, without really knowing why, she started to apologise. She said that she was tense, nervous for Derek.

'He wants more money as well, does he?' he said, rubbing his finger and thumb together.

Veronica nodded.

'They've all been in there this morning. They'll run it until the fourteenth, I suppose.'

She nodded again, embarrassed suddenly by her own feelings.

They stood in the open doorway leading to the wings and looked out over the empty stage and the rows of seats running back into the darkness, picked out by the columns of sunlight which shone through the high windows. She realised then that Devlin's position was as hopeless as her own, that he led an equally unrewarding and uncertain life on the periphery of something that might, to an outsider, have seemed enviable and exciting.

He offered her another cigarette, dropping his own to the bare boards and stepping on it. The air was filled briefly with the sharp and bitter smell of burning.

'It's a different place in summer,' he said, but without any enthusiasm. 'Holidaymakers. They'll pay to watch anything. They have discos on a Friday, June to September. They all come then. Girls, all made up, looking . . .' He hesitated. 'And on Tuesdays we have a pensioners' night. Bingo and then a sing song. The daft old fuckers pack the place out. More money than sense, most of 'em. You want to see the cars they pull up in. Sit there, they do, all singing and clapping and swaying "Daisy Daisy give me your answer do". Stupid old buggers. We used to run it into the winter at one time but we had to give it up. They stopped coming – frightened of falling on the ice or something.' He laughed at the thought.

A door slammed in the empty building and Veronica turned. Devlin watched her, returning her nervous smile.

'Downstairs,' he said.

'What?'

'That door. It'll be mighty mouse, downstairs.'

'Oh, I see.' She laughed, partly at his name for Morgan and partly in relief. The sound echoed in the empty auditorium and was reinforced by his sudden and clumsy impression of a tap dancer. She watched him banging on the naked boards, laughing and clapping, embarrassed by this childish display intended to impress her. She wanted to turn and walk away. And then, as suddenly as he had started, he stopped, the noise ebbing in a drumming which faded in the empty spaces of the room, in the ornate domed roof and along the corridor behind them.

Laughing and out of breath, he crossed the stage back to where she stood.

'Not much you can't do if you put your mind to it,' he said.

'No, I suppose not.' She wondered what he meant. She felt cold, watching her breath colour the air, lost in the tobacco smoke.

From a basket Devlin drew out a trick sword, thrusting it into his chest and pulling a face before dropping to his knees, his head level with her crotch. He fell on to his face, the sword still embedded in his chest, and lay perfectly still. She waited, watching the body and wondering for the thousandth time if there hadn't been a mistake. She studied the stage for signs of blood. She was about to prod him when he leapt to his feet, slicing the air between them with the sword.

'Never seen anybody dead before?' he asked and laughed again at her discomfort, flexing the shining silver blade.

Veronica thought briefly about her mother, the only person she ever had seen dead, laid out in the front bedroom, surrounded by neighbours, waiting downstairs in a room full of crying children. The vividness of the memory surprised her and she found herself encouraging it, closing her eyes and shutting out Devlin.

She had been nine at the time, the third eldest of four girls and two boys, dressed in a blue and white frock and shoes that had already been worn by her two older sisters. Aunts and uncles came and went, some crying, some laughing and smelling of drink. In the afternoon the house had emptied and her father had fallen asleep in his chair, the children creeping around him not knowing what to do, her youngest brother crying. It was then that she had gone upstairs to look at her mother, touching her face and pulling straight a crease in the sheet at her neck. And there, with that one precise act, the memory ended.

'. . . too much time pretending that they're something they're not.'

But she wasn't listening and told Devlin to shut up. The

unexpected harshness in her voice silenced him and he made no attempt to follow her as she left the stage.

'Too many fuckin' airs and graces, too much fuckin' . . .' she heard him shout after her.

In the corridor she met Derek. 'Well?' she asked.

'We got it.'

'How much?'

'Twenty.'

'Each?'

'Between us.'

She shook her head in disbelief.

'It was the best I could do,' he said.

She walked straight past him. He shouted after her and followed her out of the theatre into the cold sun and wet streets.

The lobsters waited calmly, their banded claws testing the air for any indication of change, sensing, perhaps, the steam condensing over them from the ovens. The crabs were less patient, barging around the trays, colliding and overturning in their attempts to escape.

Beside the ovens, uncaring or oblivious to the frantic struggles taking place beside him, stood the head chef of the Regency Hotel. The title of chef – as opposed to cook – had arrived with him. He called himself Mister David and insisted that the remainder of the staff did likewise. Only his false French accent had long since departed.

Eight women, some old, some young, one attractive, banged in and out of the swinging doors which led from the kitchen into the upstairs dining room. They wore black and white outfits, their aprons already stained with the colour of the soup (du jour, usually vegetable).

'Coppers,' one of the older women said. 'Bloody coppers: you'd think they'd have a bit more courtesy. Not a civil tongue in the lot of 'em.' The younger girls, called in to assist at such out of season functions, looked at her and then at Mister David, turning away to laugh at their own unspoken jokes.

These were Mister David's 'Ladies', his captive audience, upon whom he worked out his own frustrations and via whom he tried to impress his employers and customers alike with the delights of eating other than out of necessity.

The crabs and lobsters continued to bang and strain. They

were already dressed in French words and fancy writing on the black and gold menus.

One of the girls lifted a lobster by its fanned tail, dropping it with a squeal as it flexed in response. One by one the creatures were selected and their bands removed, stimulating a second of frantic waving and clacking before they were positioned over the pot and ceremoniously released, cracking and colouring as they fell through the water. Mister David retrieved their petrified bodies, prising open their shells and drawing out their steaming, sweet-smelling meat, mixing it before returning it to the crusts. A waitress poured sauce and stirred. Another laid wreaths of tomato, lemon and radish around each body. In the pans only the movement of the boiling water maintained the illusion of life.

Through the closed doors came the sound of applause, silence, and then laughter. Mister David clapped his hands for attention and the kitchen, frozen for a second, returned to life.

At the end of the evening the Chief Constable would ask for the waitresses to be called in. He would tell them all what a good job they had done, and lead the applause. As directed, the women would bow slightly and smile gratefully before filing back into the kitchen past Mister David, who waited to make his own separate appearance. (Initially, he had insisted that the women curtsey, but some of the older ones had difficulty with the bending and rising. Even the bowing had been a hard-fought compromise.)

Now, the speech-making began in earnest and the bursts of applause could be heard outside along the deserted Promenade.

Men slipped their ties and began to order the drinks and liqueurs not included in the price of the meal. A cream-coated policeman's helmet with a cherry on the top appeared on the table and was the source of a great many childish jokes in which the wives were encouraged to participate, laughing loyally at what their own husbands had to say and smiling sympathetically at the other wives. Later in the evening the men and women would separate and both groups would begin to enjoy themselves. Even the night's later tragedy would do little to interrupt the predictable flow of the proceedings.

'. . . and yet in a very real sense we are always policemen, whether walking the beat or the dog, playing with our kids in the park, or simply sitting at home. What the public must never be allowed to forget . . .'

A constable from Wisset Village Constabulary put his hand on the leg of his fiancée. He was drunk and she was smiling seductively at a detective sergeant, a special guest from Leeds.

'. . . and night, twenty-four hours a day. It is often said – and let there be no mistake about this, because despite what we all read and hear, and despite the media-encouraged swing towards . . .'

The timid wife of a sergeant said she had to go to the toilet. Her husband told her to wait until the end of the Chief Constable's speech. She said she didn't think she could. He told her she had no choice and turned away, joining in the brief round of applause at something he hadn't heard.

'And so it only remains for me to say a few words about the women in our lives . . .' Pause for effect.

Everyone knew what was coming.

The Wisset constable turned to his fiancée, as if to confirm that she had an important role to play in contemporary policing. She ignored him, matching the detective sergeant from Leeds move for move. Together they lifted their glasses, and later, when the dancing began, they danced together, his hands stroking her buttocks.

'Be they wives, fiancées or sweethearts, I'm sure we all appreciate the support and encouragement they give us as we do what to many may appear a thankless task.' He raised his glass. 'Gentlemen. To the ladies: our partners in crime.'

The toast was drunk. Husbands and wives looked at each other, hoping perhaps that something had changed.

Alice smiled at Norman and Norman smiled back, nodding over her shoulder to a colleague, and prouder than usual at moments like this of what he was and what he did. He told Alice what a good speech it was, as though she had not been there: how accurate and perceptive the Chief Constable's comments had been. Alice smiled and said, 'Yes,' not mentioning that it was the same speech as last year and the year before – the same speech, in fact, for as long as she could remember.

As always the meal and speeches were followed by drinking and dancing. Fat, stiff, middle-aged men pretending to be otherwise with thick moustaches and ludicrous motions which they thought to be dancing – the same few steps to every tune – their wives twirling around like drunken, corseted Flamenco dancers, lifting their skirts and sweating with the exertions.

At the back of the room the tables were dragged behind a screen and the debris of the meal was collected up into folded cloths. Claws and broken shells fell to the floor and were collected in a bucket, buried beneath uneaten potatoes and the discarded thimble-heads of prawns.

In the windows overlooking the sea, the mirrored policemen and their wives sang and danced. They saw only themselves, their own shining faces and the good time they were having.

Alice watched her eyes, keeping perfectly still and then blinking to ensure it was her own reflection she was seeing. She read the word 'Xmas' in moulded silver plastic in the glass across her chest. Beyond that, a pencil of light swept the black sea and night. She watched, hypnotised by the regular flashes and by the distance they created through the darkness. In two weeks it would be Christmas. Behind her in the glass she saw Norman, surrounded by three other non-dancing colleagues. At the head of the table the Chief Constable still held court, standing and shaking the hands of wives as they were presented to him, telling them what fine men their husbands were, as if the compliment was directed at them. Soon, she knew, Norman would insist that she too be presented and there would be no way of avoiding it. ('Lovelier than ever. Alice, of course. We're old friends, aren't we, Alice? How could I forget Alice?' A series of smiles, a hand held, the smell of tobacco and another wife being urged on from behind. 'Lovelier than ever. Marjorie, of course . . .')

Alice closed one eye, then another. Around her the noise faded, and the urge to scream, to get up and walk out, grew greater. She waited for the moment to pass, relishing the absolute silence, imagining the breaking sea, the darkness, the tiny white birds flying through it. She heard the wind, filling her head like the sound from a shell. She felt perfectly calm. She imagined herself naked, walking into the freezing waves, the line of footprints filling behind her, washing away, leaving her invisible, untraceable. She moved slowly through the water, feeling its weight against her legs and arms and chest . . .

'Alice, love, you all right? Not tired are you, love?' It was Norman. He was looking at his watch to signify that the answer to his last question should be no.

Alice opened her eyes, saw him and smiled.

'Y Viva España. Oh this year I'm off to sunny Spain.' The dancers were singing, moving in and out of a wide circle, towards and away from each other, holding hands and then clapping above their heads. 'España por favor!' Even the men with whom Norman was speaking were tapping their feet and holding up their glasses to the dancers to let them know that they too were enjoying themselves.

Alice watched them, turning once more to look at the silver 'Xmas', the darkness and the shining light beyond.

Outside, the birds in the harbour rose together, screaming at the intrusion of a fire engine, its colours shining in the wet and its bell breaking the night's silence as it sped along the Promenade, its blue running light reflected in a hundred empty windows.

Devlin sat on a trunk in the narrow corridor. At his feet stood the basket of rabbits, their ears flat, noses pressed to the mesh. He studied his watch, mouthing words to himself. On the stage he saw the midget run from one screen to another, heard the screams and shouts of the children. His mind was not on the pantomime.

Ten o'clock. They were running twenty minutes late. He turned to look out of the half-open fire exit at the far end of the corridor, seeing only an oblong of darkness and hearing the muffled sound of music, of people dancing and singing.

The woman in the leotard left the dressing room and paused to stand beside him, ready to make her entrance. He ignored her, his eyes fixed on the open door and the darkness beyond. She turned to look and caught the flash of the distant lighthouse. Then she felt the draught and complained. Devlin looked up with a start, as though he had only just realised she was there. She asked him what he was waiting for. He said nothing, slammed the door shut and moved along the corridor away from her.

In the darkness, on the road beyond the village, Devlin's mother died in her sleep, asphyxiated by smoke and choking fumes as her home burned around her in explosions of cracking wood and burning tins.

Outside, neighbours stood in the rain, watching as the flimsy construction fell apart. No one knew whether or not the chalet had been empty.

An explosion blew two cans into the air. A woman screamed and the crowd backed away, walking through the saturated grass and thinking about their own, equally combustible homes.

Every ten seconds the beam of yellow light lit up the scene. The neighbouring fields with their crops of caravans were also briefly and starkly illuminated.

And then, with the final collapse which blew the sparks high into the air, the fire died.

It was now that the fire engine arrived and completed the job of the rain. The men moved through the wreckage in their yellow waterproofs, chopping at the blackened wood and kicking it to the ground.

One of them stopped, and after a series of whispered messages the onlookers were marshalled firmly towards the opposite side of the lane.

4

LOST. Summerfield Road Area.
Ginger Kitten. Red Collar. Ring
44718. REWARD.
D. Good Luck and Fondest Wishes,
B.
TRACEY. Please Come Home. We
All Miss You. Mother Ill with
Worry. Love Dad.

Twelve days before Christmas the sun shone on the town.
Yellow on the sea and with some real warmth for a whole
morning. With it came the shoppers, and in the market the
stallholders increased their yelling as time ran out. People
carried Christmas trees held in shape by nylon bags, and fruit
shops sold wreaths of evergreen and holly.

'Mother Sick with Worry' is what he had originally written,
the man at the newspaper suggesting that the 'Sick' be changed to
'Ill'. Similarly, he added 'We All' to the clipped 'Miss You' and
'Love' to 'Dad'.

The appeal had been the idea of a neighbour, well-meaning
but insistent, who could not believe that a fourteen-year-old
child would want to spend Christmas away from her home and
family, and was certain that such an appeal would prove fruitful.
(Had she been alive, Tracey would by now have been fifteen.)
The appeal was inserted, three nights running, in the personal
column, largely neglected, but which on this occasion also
included the lost kitten, a printer's mistake from the Lost and
Founds.

At the desk the man had re-written the message and calculated
the cost. The neighbour had suggested that the paper would
probably insert the appeal free. Tracey's father mentioned this,
and after a brief meeting with someone in another office, the man
returned smiling and said that they'd be only too pleased. A
gesture. As he re-wrote the words on to the correct form he
asked if there had been any news of the girl, any indication of
where she might be. He spoke without looking up, nodding
and saying 'I see, I see' to her father's lengthy and uncertain

response. When the message was written and read back the conversation was at an end.

As all this was taking place, Norman entered the office and approached the desk waving a sheet of paper containing brief details of the local court cases heard the previous week. These would be printed under the heading 'Brief Cases', and dealt largely with motoring offences and disorderly behaviour when drunk. Placing the sheet carefully into a basket marked 'Police/Council' he nodded to the two men and waved to a woman who passed behind them carrying a tray of cups. He recognised the girl's father but did not stop to talk. To Norman the girl was still simply missing, soon to return. To her father she was the cause of his temporary celebrity and of his wife's deteriorating condition. 'Mother Ill with Worry' masked the slide towards mental exhaustion and breakdown.

Outside, Norman turned his face to the sun and walked briskly back towards his waiting car and partner.

Three days later the ginger kitten with its red collar was found dead in a disused yard. The woman who found it knew nothing of the advertisement or reward. And so, like the missing girl, the kitten remained missing. And, undiscovered, it too gave hope where none should have existed and kept alive the possibility of its return.

'No, the thing about a body is that if it's kept whole, not dismembered or anything, then there's very little chance of it remaining undetected for long. Rates of decomposition, see. You can't tell me that anyone could come within, say, ten yards of a corpse and not know it was there. All down to decomposition, see, and its associated . . . associated . . .' Norman waved his hand, uncertain of what he wanted to say.

Around the table the others responded with little interest.

Norman was convinced that there was a good deal of truth, or if not truth then at least common sense, in what he was saying. And what he didn't know he masked with spiralling hand gestures and knowing looks, convincing himself at least that what he said could not be disputed.

'Associated what?' Morgan asked, timing his question for effect.

But Norman had expected this and ignored the remark with a practised glance.

They sat around the table, waiting. Alice was in the kitchen preparing pudding. The previous evening's paper had reported the fire on the lighthouse road and had once again made reference to the missing girl, calling one a tragedy the other a disaster. The police, it suggested, were growing concerned. Morgan lowered the paper and was about to speak.

'Growing concerned, it says. That's all.' Veronica was tired of the topic and irritated by Morgan's constant goading of Norman.

Vincent smiled – partly at the predictability of what was happening, partly at Rita, who smiled back simply because she hadn't been listening and thought a joke had been told.

Norman explained to them all what was meant by 'Growing concerned'. 'Like "Helping with enquiries" or "New developments". We're trained to use those kind of phrases. We use them because it makes things easier. It's what the public want to hear. It's only the same as, er, as legal jargon – stuff like "Aggravated assault" or—'

'Indecent assault.' Morgan grinned around the table.

'Exactly.' Norman sat back and smiled at them each in turn. Derek, he knew, would agree with him, and so to maintain the momentum of his winning argument he said: 'Isn't that right, Derek?'

'Me? I, er . . . well, I've never really thought about it like that, but I suppose it's best all round.'

Veronica turned slowly to stare at her husband, causing him to feel instantly guilty for being so weak.

'Well, I think they ought to tell us what they really think has happened to her,' Rita said. 'What if she's been – been – like you said – assaulted—?'

'Indecently assaulted.'

'What then?'

Norman smiled again and shook his head. 'And what if we said that and then she went and turned up the next day? We don't deal in half truths and guesses – can't afford to . . .'

In the kitchen Alice heard him repeat what the Chief Constable had said two nights previously.

'We work from facts, solid facts, indisputable evidence – and at present that means that the girl's still missing. And because of the amount of time she's been missing our concern for her safety and eventual return is growing. Like it says – "Growing concerned".'

'She could have been killed and dumped in the sea. Fish food,' Morgan said.

Veronica said: 'Do you mind!' and watched the white balls of fat form in the cold gravy around her plate.

'We'd know if that had happened soon enough. Tides round here bring everything back in two days maximum. She'd have washed up down the coast, Fairsthorpe at the furthest. Not much chance of her being undiscovered if she had.'

Derek said that he supposed every force in the country would have her description by now.

'Every single one,' Norman said proudly. 'Description, photograph, the lot. She'll turn up. And when she does . . .'

The conversation oscillated between the likelihood of the girl's return and the discovery of her mutilated body. Norman was about to say something on the subject of forensic chemistry (about which he knew very little, the name itself being his prop against ignorance), when Alice entered with a jug of custard and asked everyone if the meal had been to their liking. Morgan was the only one to reply, saying that he preferred his meat less well done and peas to carrots, but that he wasn't complaining.

'Don't stop your talking on my account,' said Alice. 'Just pretend I'm not here. What was it? The weather? Christmas?'

'Forensic chemistry,' announced Norman, surprising them all.

'What?'

'Oh, I—'

'Thousands go missing every year. Right, Norm?' Vincent waited.

'Yes, thousands.' He tried to remember the exact number of thousands, but could not. 'Mind you, once they're over eighteen then there's very little we can do about it.'

With his finger Morgan collected the ball of custard which threatened to drip from the spout of the jug. Rita saw him, relieved that Derek, and not she, was the next to use it.

Alice returned, this time to clear a space on the crowded table for a tray of cups and a teapot. Her presence once again checked the conversation.

Norman informed them all that he had seen an ambulance and police car heading towards where the fire had been. Vincent asked Alice if she had enjoyed the dinner dance. Norman stopped speaking to listen to her answer.

Alice shivered, touched the front of her lemon-coloured cardigan and told them that someone had just walked over her grave.

No one spoke. Then Vincent told her she ought to sit down, that she did too much.

Alice said they weren't to worry, that she felt perfectly all right and that there was no rest for the wicked. With this she left the room, leaving them all wondering what she meant and trying to remember what they had been talking about before she came in. Through the kitchen doorway, Vincent saw her grip a chair and cover her face with her hand.

'Forensic chemistry,' Norman said, and nothing more.

'They blow up fat, bodies at sea, and the birds eat their eyes.' Morgan began to laugh and moved his spoon through the air like a scavenging bird.

5

Alice and Rita walked together through the market, two lines of stalls along each side of the road. In winter there was only one market day each week, offering fruit and vegetables, scented towels, cheap electrical goods, car accessories, second-hand books and homemade pastries and bread. The stall selling see-through Christmas wrapping paper, four sheets for ten pence, was doing the briskest trade.

'Five sheets for ten last year,' Alice whispered to Rita, not wanting the man to overhear. 'Probably buys it penny a sheet.'

Rita nodded.

Naked bulbs hung along the shaky scaffolding of the stalls. There was Japanese writing on the boxes of remote-controlled toys displayed as 'Excellent Presents for Boys, Giveaway Prices'. Mounds of chestnuts spilled past satsumas and sprouts into the deep blue tissue paper which lined the gutter.

At the end of the market stood the chip van, blowing steam and filling the air with sweet and acid smells. The traders shouted to each other and joked with their customers, hurriedly wrapping shoes and leather belts, while assuring them that they couldn't buy cheaper and that they, personally, were losing money on each item sold.

The two women paused at each stall. Alice, adopting the role of Mother, pointed out all the best buys and the shoddy goods to be avoided. She bought three cotton handkerchiefs for fifty pence. That, she announced proudly, was a real bargain, one of the few. Rita smiled, followed her round and offered to carry her shopping bag, spilling with potatoes and awkward silver foil. Better to get two packets, Alice had said. You never knew with turkeys, and the man on the stall couldn't guarantee that he'd have any left the week after. 'Bargain, see, two for a quid. Too good to resist. Two, darling? Thanks.' Rita looked on at the man's easy flattery of the nondescript housewives who bought his foil. She smiled too as Alice pretended not to enjoy her turn for this kind of attention. First he admired her coat, now he pretended to mistake her and Rita for sisters. But Alice held out.

Was the foil damaged in any way, she wanted to know. Would he do that to them? Honestly! Try to make an honest living . . .

Alice and Rita stood behind a woman who held a dress to the broad back of a friend, demanding of the Pakistani stallholder to see something similar in a size sixteen. 'All I have on the rack,' he said, smiling whitely, his hands together in a prayer. 'Red's not my colour, you see,' said the woman. 'Turquoise, that's me.' 'Red's not her colour,' her friend echoed. 'Not your colour, is it, Jean?' The man pressed his hands still closer together and let his smile slip. He replaced the dress in its cellophane sleeve and put it back on the rack. He turned to the other women who inspected his box of novelty underwear, laughing with them and making jokes about their husbands which, coming from a Pakistani, some of them did not take kindly to. Others bought the underwear as presents, listing the names of uncles and brothers and giggling over the lewd designs and messages.

The two women looking for a dress had turned their attention to a stall of shoes, searching for something in a six with buckles. 'They're you, love. Could have been made special. Not to worry, soon loosen up a bit. Ten? Nine to you. Can't say fairer.' 'What do you think, Jean?'

Walking with Alice and carrying her shopping gave Rita an unaccustomed feeling of calm. She smiled at the women to whom she was introduced – other landladies, neighbours. Of them all, she realised, she alone was immune to the flattery they had come to feed on. At the vegetable stall, Alice asked her opinion of the oranges and she gave it, the words coming before she had time to consider what she was saying. Alice agreed with her. And the lettuces? 'Still a bit expensive.' And not as crisp as they could be.

This was all Rita had ever wanted: to be able to express an opinion and to have it accepted was, to her, a precious novelty. She bought a bunch of three bananas, testing them and looking over the remainder of the display as though about to buy more.

At one stall hung a line of pigeons and rabbits, their matted heads in plastic bags solid with blood. 'Seasonal Greetings. Join Our Next Year's Xmas Club NOW.' The animals were flanked on either side by holly leaves and cardboard angels.

Beside the chip van a crowd had gathered, and above the noise Alice heard the staccato crackling of a police radio. Like a baby's scream, the noise was designed to cut through all others. A young constable walked calmly and authoritatively through the shoppers. A woman had fainted, her shopping spilled between her legs. Other women collected it up for her. The young policeman knelt and spoke into his radio. One of the stallholders pointed out that the woman on the ground was the mother of the missing girl. A surge of sympathy rose from the crowd and they moved closer, an added attraction, all saying what a shame it was, poor thing, out of her mind with worry, taking it badly. And now this . . . One of the women pointed out that there was a purse, with money in it, among the spilled shopping. Perhaps the policeman ought to hang on to it until . . .

Alice and Rita stood at the edge of the crowd. Rita tried to see, but Alice turned away.

'Another wild goose chase if you ask me.' Norman's partner took the packet of cigarettes from his cap, lit one and filled the car with smoke.

Norman wound down his window and shone a torch through the wire mesh into the dark, strongly scented enclosure.

'Still see the stars,' the driver said, and Norman pointed the torch upwards, up past the Kiddies Korner Zoo sign and into the black dome above them, tracing the powerful beam into the branches of a naked tree. Smoke flowed over his shoulders and out into the cold morning air.

'Sunrise at 7.44,' Norman said.

'Bloody hell! That's an hour and ten minutes yet.'

Norman looked at his watch. 'Hour and fourteen.'

The man swore again. 'Let's face it, we're not likely to see anything out there, are we?'

Norman didn't answer, turning away to trace the base of the enclosure with the ball of yellow light.

'We'll give it till seven,' the man said. 'And then we'll drive round to the beach huts. Another one broken up last night.' As he spoke he looked past Norman into the darkness and wished he'd been scheduled to come with someone else.

Without the heater the car became quickly cold, only the yellow lines and numbers of the radio suggesting any warmth. Along each side of the narrow road the grass stood white and stiff with frost, reflecting the light like rows of teeth.

Beyond the road the square outline of Sarraby Hall was clearly visible against the grey sky. Open to the public from

April to September, the house was now cold and empty, the wind plucking at the flakes of loose stucco the council workmen would replace in the spring. The ornamental gardens had been reduced to acres of wet grass and empty flower beds. Beyond the house the grass sloped to the edge of the cliffs. From there it was possible to look back over the whole of the town and to see the coast with its crescent of sand stretching towards Spurn Point, almost forty miles away. On clear days the line of the land faded to nothing, but now all that could be seen from the cliff was the illuminated street pattern of the town below and the first house lights of the early risers. There might also have been the lights of a fishing boat trawling the bay or returning home along the coast. To the north stood the lighthouse with its ring of white houses.

Occasionally the silence was broken by one of the exotic birds sitting out the winter in the dry warmth of the Bird House.

'Wind the window up, Norm, or we'll both bloody freeze to death.' The man replaced his cap and studied his mouth in the rear-view mirror.

'I think we ought to have a walk round towards the Snack Bar. If anything—'

'Walk round? Bloody hell, you want us to get out of the car and start traipsing through all that bloody grass? We'd get soaked. It's only half past six.'

'Twenty to—'

'Half past six and bloody freezing! Look. You can see for yourself. And besides which, there's caretakers, keepers, that sort of thing. If the girl had shown up here we'd have known about it. Let's face it, Norm, she'll have spent the one night up at the chalet and then she'll have been off. It stands to reason. She's miles away by now. Probably living it up somewhere. What's she going to hang around here for? Ask yourself that. If she was anywhere within ten – no, twenty miles, then she'd have been picked up and brought back home. And everybody would have been happy and we wouldn't be sat here looking for the stupid little—' He banged his fist against the wheel and turned away.

The shapes of wooden buildings and trees emerged from the darkness. Behind them a line of white arc lights lit up the car park and marked the line of the road. The lights added to the frozen scene, reflecting broken ice in the puddles.

'Used to bring the kids out here when they were a bit younger.

Bring a picnic and watch the deers and kangaroos. Then we had
that goat that somebody killed. Remember?'

Norman nodded.

'Funny looking buggers. Three horns, some of them. More. If
you ask—'

The radio burst noisily into the car, interrupting what he was
about to say. He picked it up and went through the routine of
identification with complete disinterest.

A woman's voice repeated what he said and clicked into
silence.

Then they spoke of Christmas. Mostly the driver spoke, but
Norman added a few words, clicking his torch on and off
through the windscreen.

Less than an hour later, at Norman's insistence, they left the
car and walked towards the wire mesh of the enclosure. Norman
searched it, swinging the torch from side to side. Two marbles of
amber light shone back and something moved across the beam.

'*There*,' the man shouted, pointing uncertainly into the darkness. 'Was it a deer, a goat?' There was no place in his guessing
for the girl.

Norman moved the beam of light in the direction of the
animal. The man moved closer, looking over his shoulder.
'There was definitely something. I saw it. Certain.'

This time, two pairs of eyes shone back at them. One pair
moved away, but the other remained immobile, staring back.

'It's a kangaroo!' the man shouted, causing the animal to rise
up on to its hind legs in fright. It stood watching him now,
propped upright against the mesh.

Norman shone the torch on to the cream fur of its belly and
took a step forward.

'Watch it, Norm, I've seen them buggers on the telly. Break a
man's leg with one blow of its tail. You just be careful and . . .'
He took two paces backwards.

Beyond the enclosure a light appeared in one of the downstairs rooms of the house. Above it, the grey sky was already
marbled with other colours as the sun began to rise over the sea.
A bird whistled and was answered by the drawn out rattle of
another.

'It's a wallaby,' Norman announced.

'A what?'

'Wallaby.'

'What are they, then? Just small kangaroos, I thought.'
'Same family. Some are nearly as big. Some—'
'Australia!'
'Yes, Australia and Tasmania. No kangaroos in Tasmania, only wallabies.'
'Oh.'

Norman stared at the animal. If his partner had not been standing behind him he would have spoken to it. Watching it, he too forgot about the missing girl and the reason for their visit. The wallaby watched him, still chewing, and raised itself to the height of his chest. Behind it, others moved through the darkness, thumping over the frozen ground.

'Red-necked wallaby,' Norman said to himself.

The animal made a sudden choking sound before dropping back on to all fours and turning away. Norman saw the balls of droppings which filled the compound and then the outlines of the other animals as they pressed together against the cold. He was distracted briefly by the distant outline of the town and by the strings of light which disappeared as entire streets were plunged back into the waiting darkness. When he turned back he saw that the animals had moved away to the far corner of the compound. He turned off his torch and nothing but their outlines remained.

In a bar, glass half-empty, early afternoon, carols on the radio, Rita met a man who ran a freak show, closed for the winter, but painted and opened in April to display a mummified skeleton, the world's smallest man (in reality the wizened and preserved body of a baby gibbon minus tail), and a three-headed pig from Hereford, all stuffed or moulded in wax, and all untouchable beneath glass in a single dark room. The holidaymakers who paid to see the exhibits invariably complained at the obvious stitching by which the pig's two additional heads were attached, but because they had half expected to be disappointed before entering, seldom insisted on their money back; it was a precarious balance from which the man made his living.

'What do they expect for ten bob? Right price, see.' The man explained what he meant. Just enough for him to make a decent living during the season but not too much for them to get too upset when they actually saw the forged exhibits. The fact that the mummified corpse was still firmly encrusted in dirty bandages only served to arouse their suspicions, but by the time they had reached the world's only Siamese Triplets (a faded sepia photograph of three long-skirted women holding tennis racquets and smiling in opposite directions), the customers were usually too busy laughing at their own incredulity to be really serious about demanding a refund.

The man gave Rita a card upon which his name was printed alongside a drawing of a shrunken head. From his pocket he pulled a rubber replica – topped with shining horse hair and with a brass ring through its nose.

'Very popular. Hang them in cars.'

Rita said she'd take his word for it and drank the drink he had bought her.

'Had a wax model of a local rapist at one time. Late fifties, it was. His actual suit and everything. Killed this woman with a hammer and then – had to take it out, though – offensive to the relatives, see.' There was genuine disappointment in his voice.

Rita nodded, and the man said it was a great shame and that it would have been a good attraction for the coming season. He went on to tell her of the various animals he had exhibited, all with malformed or additional limbs or heads, and of the small shark with the shoe in its stomach. Family business, he explained – his father's before him and all that. As he spoke, she got the impression that given the opportunity he would abandon the freaks and make his living selling second-hand cars.

He showed her a book of trick matches in which a man's pink and red rubber penis sprang to attention when opened. He laughed, repeating the trick and telling her how popular it was, only twenty pence. She smiled, still too sober to laugh with him. He touched her arm and whispered about a pickled bull's . . . (he never actually said the word, winking and nodding at the matches until she understood). 'Had it in a big long jar like one of them spaghetti things,' he said, drawing his hands apart.

She closed the matches and slid them towards him.

'Brings out the worst in people,' he said.

'What?'

'Freaks, stuff like that.'

'Oh. Yes, I suppose it does.'

'They all pretend to feel sorry, disgusted, but in the end they all want to have a look.' His explanation petered out. After a few minutes' silence he raised his glass and said, 'Cheers'.

Rita said, 'Cheers,' and the man waited until she lifted her glass before drinking from his own.

'Had a three-legged chicken, once. Only a chick, really. Five days old. Had this extra foot growing out of its knee. Didn't actually touch the ground or walk on it. Died.' He shook his head at the thought. 'Five days old and it died. Fit as a fiddle one minute, every chance that all three legs might grow longer . . . and then it just died. Came down one morning and there it was, dead. Died in the night, see, and I'd already paid to have the posters drawn up. We managed to put it in the show for a few days afterwards and put it in the fridge at night. But then it began to go off and this woman complained.'

Rita, who hadn't really been listening, looked over his shoulder to a television mounted above the bar, on which a line of horses ran a race in perfect silence. A group of drinkers stood beneath it and watched. When the race finished one of the men punched the air and cheered. The others shook their heads and turned away.

'You tend to get a lot of dogs with deformities for some reason.'

'What?'

'Dogs.'

'Oh, yes.'

As the man spoke, he played with the matches, studying the mechanism, oblivious to what a few minutes ago he had found so funny. He spoke without looking up, as though he might have said it all a thousand times before.

'Dogs and pigs,' he went on. 'Dogs and pigs are always good for an extra head or something.'

They left together. It rained only intermittently and lightly, and as they walked, Rita could feel her hand against the man's side, held in by his arm.

Alice left the theatre and walked home along the Promenade. The tide was out, leaving the beach to the bait diggers who, even at that late hour, searched by torch light for the tell-tale scribbled casts of buried worms, their progress marked by the mounds of sand behind them. They shouted to each other and their dogs, their torch beams stretching and disappearing across the open space.

She stood and watched them, wondering at the effort required and at the large piles of sand thrown up in the search for a solitary worm. Then she closed her eyes, content simply to feel the cold air with its edge of ice and salt against her face.

Away to her left, the theatre remained outlined in strings of light, the broken sound of an organ still audible. Behind her closed eyelids she saw the points of coloured light and the outline of the dome.

Throughout their stay, Derek and the others had kept suggesting that she should go and see the show. Pantomimes were for children, she told them. Rubbish! She deserved a night out. Wasn't that right, Norman? Well . . . of course it was. The two tickets had been propped against the mantelpiece for over a month – a permanent reminder of her link with her lodgers and of the separate world they inhabited.

And tonight she had gone. Norman was on the evening shift and she had gone alone, smiling nervously at the children and their parents who queued around her, wanting to explain why she was there without children or grandchildren of her own.

In the foyer she had spotted Morgan in a lurex cape and pointed wizard's cap selling programmes. She had pretended not to see him, looking instead at the details on her ticket and searching the semi-circle of doors for the right one. But he had seen her, had strutted across the maroon-carpeted hall and had made a great fuss of giving her a free programme. She had taken it reluctantly, smiling apologetically at the people standing around her. When he reached up for her hand, she allowed him to lead her through the crowd towards the appropriate door. 'Make way! Make way!' She felt strangely flattered and tugged at her collar, holding her white gloves and nodding politely at the people who moved aside to let them through. Like royalty, she thought. Like royalty making an entrance. Children pointed and were told not to be rude. Mothers smiled at her.

In the darkness of the corridor skirting the auditorium, Morgan removed his pointed hat and released her hand. Now she felt awkward, abandoned, as though she had been the victim of some kind of deceit.

'Very full,' she said. 'Lots of people.'

'Makes no difference. We get paid the same full or empty.'

He replaced his hat, standing with his back to her, allowing her to smooth out the creases from his cape.

'Lovely material.'

Morgan felt it, as though checking what she said. 'It's all right.'

'No, it's nice.' She took a step back as if to admire him.

'A 3,' he said loudly. 'You're in the balcony.' He handed back her ticket and walked ahead of her along the corridor, his cape flashing under the wall lights. She followed him, vaguely aware that she had in some way upset him. She wanted to apologise but knew that that would only make matters worse. So instead she followed him, counting the letters and numbers on the doors they passed. Ahead of them, one of the doors opened and two fat children ran out. One of them, a girl, held a five-pound note above her head and the other, a boy, demanded his share. The sound of their running drummed in the confined space. Through the open doorway, Alice saw a man wiping his forehead with a handkerchief. On the wall around him she saw rows of framed portraits. The door swung shut and she walked quickly towards where Morgan waited at the foot of some stairs. Behind her the tide of parents and children had started to flow along the corridor towards them.

She had enjoyed the show, had applauded vigorously at every opportunity and at one point had even found herself shouting, her voice lost in the rising crescendo of screaming children around her. She felt encouraged and exhilarated.

Now, outside, she looked down from the Promenade at the men on the beach and at the trail of disturbed sand behind them. She saw the white shapes of the birds, awaiting the water's return. Someone shouted and she saw a beam of light sweep towards her, disappearing as it climbed the concave wall, outlining the railings to her left and right. The buttons on her coat shone. She heard the men laughing and the banging of their spades as they moved away.

A procession of cars passed behind her, each circling the one-way system of the Promenade before disappearing into the night.

She turned away from the sea and walked home. At midnight Norman would return to sit for twenty minutes in front of the fire with a hot drink before coming up to bed. She would listen to the indistinct and familiar noises made by the others: the sounds of running water, loose boards, shoes falling, voices: reassuring sounds. Once, she had dreamt of a house overrun with children and had woken to the sound of beds and doors and subdued shouting.

Almost home, she turned and saw the outline of the theatre disappear a line at a time until all that remained was the dome and crowning spotlight, hovering in the darkness like a flying saucer. Then that vanished too, and the building might never have existed, not even its outline discernible against the night sky.

In the darkness, protected against the cold and only a few minutes from home, she felt strangely elated, inexplicably happy, and relieved, as if a fear had been dispelled.

Perhaps tonight she would wait up for Norman and the others. Perhaps she might even go to see the show again and sit again amongst the rows of shouting children.

6

The trees surrounding the Crematorium and Garden of Rest had all been savagely pruned at the end of the previous summer by a gang of council workmen sawing at them from the open top of a double-decker bus. They had moved from tree to tree, shouting and swearing, laughing and singing. The driver had remained in his cab as the branches dropped around him and as the sawdust fell in a spout from the braying saws, their notes rising and falling as the branches gave. Mounds of wood and leaves filled the pavement like culled animals awaiting collection. The trees were reduced to stumps, a fence of deformed hands and fists around the open space with its tiny squares of black and white marble, grass and pink gravel walkways.

Relatives of the Dead, as is often considered their duty, complained. One said the Dead ought to be left in peace, enclosed and hidden from the Living – not open to view and to vandalism. The newspaper called the trees 'Butchered Stumps' and 'Symbols of the Council's Insensitivity'. A line of saplings appeared, each with its wooden stake and caliper of wire and rubber.

Now, at the service for Florence Devlin, the trees remained lifeless, leaving those mourning and celebrating her death uncomfortably exposed to the passing shoppers and traffic.

From the gentle slope in which the dead were interred, it was possible to look down over the entire town, through the outline of the harbour and out over the sea with its blemish of running shadows.

Devlin swore at the long grass which brushed against the trousers of his only suit and ran a finger around his sleeve where the armband pinched. It had been nine days since the fire, nine days alone with his grief. There had been no reason for a detailed medical examination and only cursory inspections by both police and fire brigade. After the fire another call went up for the demolition of the chalets. The angry letters amused him, as did a great deal else about the way people had behaved towards him since his mother's death. The sympathy and concern were yet further indications of his immunity and cunning. Two crimes, two murders and not a word said or a finger pointed. The chief fire officer had said that the disaster was long overdue and that he had been predicting something like it for years. Rather than seeking to expose him, the authorities seemed to be actually protecting him. He, and not his mother, had become the victim of the fire.

Six relatives were all that remained – three sisters and their husbands, all his mother's age, all of whom impressed upon him the cost in time and money of their presence. It was a morning service and they would be leaving as soon as possible afterwards. This suited Devlin, who accepted their sympathy and insincere offers of help. Perhaps he should have asked them all for some cash to tide him over? What would they say then, in front of each other, in front of the vicar?

A wisp of smoke rose and then fell from the chimney of the crematorium. The wind tugged at its edges, pulling it into horns before dispersing it.

Florence had been cremated at a brief and clinical service. Only Devlin had attended.

Under the circumstances, and considering the state of the deceased, cremation had seemed the wisest alternative, recommended by the undertaker who had made the arrangements. Now she was firmly installed in a brick wall dotted with plaques and empty terracotta bowls. An indecipherable inscription ran the length of the wall, chiselled out in strange letters which Devlin was happy to ignore, but which her sisters and their husbands studied, mispronouncing the words and nodding at their solemn, unguessed meaning.

One of the women had begun to cry – more at another memory than at the loss of Florence – and the others turned to each other in surprise.

She shook, dabbing at her face with the sleeve of her coat. She apologised and the others said they understood.

'Only natural, after all,' Devlin said, and the men were unable any longer to conceal their anger at his callousness. One by one they turned away and, as they left, passed the brick in which Florence was contained, touching it in a final gesture of respect. The simple act released them from the morbidity of the occasion and allowed them to move more quickly back to their waiting cars.

Devlin walked behind them, ignored now except for the three parting handshakes and three cold kisses. No one asked what he would do with himself now that he was alone, and no one cared.

Turning, he walked down the gentle hill into the town. His offer of a farewell drink had been refused and he had regretted asking. Pulling off his armband, he began to whistle.

On the night of Saturday, the eighteenth of December, a storm of gale-force winds raced towards the coast over the dark sea, driving like a wave into the town and leaving a trail of damage in its wake.

In the harbour, red flags pulled taut and the smaller boats rocked and swung at their moorings, their sides scraping. Above them the lifeboat waited. Three of the boats were smashed, two against the harbour wall, where they rose on the incoming swell, fell and disappeared. The third boat was lifted out of the water and deposited against the protective railings, each wave punching at it until it too was smashed and scattered.

Lines of empty light sockets fell from their posts, trailing across the Promenade. Adjoining roads were flooded as the sea rose in a froth, curling back from the granite walls where the wind slashed horizontally against the empty summer houses and beach huts, battened against the winter.

Out in the North Sea, a trawler from Hull was sunk with the loss of three lives, two of them eighteen-year-olds on their first trip, thirty miles from home. In Sunderland a man died when a falling tree guillotined his car. 'Million to One Chance Tragedy,' the papers called it.

The storm tore through the town, plucking slates and aerials, threatening trees and spinning the Christmas decorations strapped above shop doorways.

At four in the morning the wind began to fall and the tide turned. By six the streets were drying and the boats in the harbour floating back into position with the retreating water.

People began to inspect the damage, assessing costs and insisting that something be done to protect them in the future. A yellow lorry stood abandoned in the centre of the town, its sacks of potatoes torn open, their contents rolling along the gutters like fleeing rats.

Two policemen stood beside one of the smashed boats, kicking at the pieces and shaking their heads at what had happened.

On the Promenade a man in wellingtons nailed sheets of hardboard over the broken glass of his shop window. At Sarraby Hall, four rabbits had been crushed beneath the bricks and timber of their collapsing hutch. A leg was broken in a motor accident caused by flooding, and two people were hit by flying debris.

Everyone was talking about the storm. Some had sat up through the night, watching their reflections warp as the glass in their windows bowed under pressure. In the allotments the sheets of plastic covering the sheds sucked in and out like the breathing of old, asthmatic men.

By eight the sun was shining and a procession of War Veterans went ahead as planned between the town's two war memorials. The marchers were accompanied by several bands and the Salvation Army. A born-again Christian marched alongside the leaders wearing a sandwich-board. The marchers wore their medals on their overcoats and attempted unsuccessfully to walk in time with the music. People stopped to watch, wondering why they bothered. The wives of some of the men walked alongside their husbands and the leader carried a wreath.

Fur-coated old women filed out of a church, only pausing to smile at the vicar as they walked unsteadily past the graves, like bears fresh from hibernation. Husbands and sons held the doors of waiting cars, turning to watch the marching men.

On the beach a crowd gathered around a dead shark abandoned by the tide, its eyes already eaten, its white belly open and stinking. Photographs were taken and dogs examined the corpse, licking its sand-coated flanks. Above the crowd hovered the confetti of gulls, drawn from the sewer pipe by the promise of this richer prize.

Alice inspected her garden for signs of damage, walking backwards into the road to check for lost slates. Norman was on duty, six until two – probably later, he had warned her as he dressed by the glow of the bedside lamp. Probably later on account of the storm damage.

Even then the winds were beginning to fall. Alice had watched him as he dressed, watched him in triplicate in the mirrors of the dressing table, and then in silhouette as he turned out the light and crossed the room, telling her, as usual, to go back to sleep. She listened to him without answering, threatened by the wind but reassured by his presence, his inflexible routine.

Vincent, after a month of near desperation, had found work washing cars on the forecourt of a used-car showroom. Up and down the same used, unsold and unsellable cars five days a week. ('Don't rub too hard on the wings of the Escort and watch the passenger door of the Imp.') It was not Vincent's idea of rehabilitation.

After a week he left and began working with a man who travelled around the region with a market stall, setting up in the town each Wednesday. He sold whatever he could sell: steering wheel covers, handkerchiefs, yellow and blue synthetic toys ('Cuddly Bears – Spoil the Kids'), quartz watches with plastic straps, £2.99.

At first the man treated Vincent like a customer; nothing was too good for him. After their first day together he gave him one of the watches and a pile of tea towels printed with views of York Minster. Vincent gave the towels to Alice, and the watch he showed to everyone as evidence of his ability to get on, and of his employer's dependence upon him.

Mr Berryman was known in the town as something of an eccentric, a poster in his window proclaiming that JESUS SAVES COMPLETELY when you come to him through GOD. A sticker in the rear window of his car said the same. Sometimes Vincent washed the car as a favour and Mr Berryman said he had never seen it looking so good, that he had forgotten what colour it was underneath all the dirt.

Vincent read the messages and thought about them. 'A lamb returned to the fold, you could be, Vincent,' Mr Berryman had told him, his arm around Vincent's shoulder. 'More joy in one repenting sinner than in . . . than in . . .' He had said it when drunk one afternoon as they stood together at the stall. Later, reinforced by the flask which he kept patting, Mr Berryman had stood on an upturned box and shouted his messages about Jesus to the assembled shoppers. He supported himself by holding Vincent's shoulders. Vincent had been embarrassed, smiling at the passers-by, who looked up at Mr Berryman as he waved his arms and threatened to fall, and passed by much more quickly. The other stallholders had dragged him down, fed him from his flask and explained to Vincent that it sometimes took him like that, and that it was nothing to worry about. For the remainder of the afternoon, Vincent had managed the stall single-handedly, his every sale praised by Mr Berryman who sat behind him singing softly about the coming of the Lord and Gentle Jesus, meek and mild.

'You see, I don't think women – well, Alice anyway – I don't think they really understand about soil, about how finely balanced a, er, compound it really is.' Norman stood with his face to the sea, his foot resting on the railings. On one side of him stood Derek; on the other, Vincent. It was Sunday afternoon and, as usual, the walk had been Norman's idea.

'Yes. I mean no. I suppose so,' Derek said, not really certain of the answer expected or if one was even necessary.

'No feel for it, you see. No real involvement. Nearest most of them come to it is on fresh vegetables.' Norman laughed at his own joke. 'What about you, Vincent?'

To Vincent it was just dirt, but enthusiasm was required.

'Needs looking after,' he said, at once both profound and noncommittal. He resented Norman's reference to his sister. Why bother to include her? Why not just say 'women'?

'Exactly. My point exactly. What they don't seem to realise is that you only get out of the soil what you're prepared to put into it. It's as simple as that.'

'Fertiliser, you mean?' Derek said, turning his back on the sea and wind.

'Fertiliser, time, energy, effort. Proper care and attention – that's what it needs. You can't go on taking all the time without putting something back. Stands to reason.'

Both Derek and Vincent wondered where the conversation was leading. Couldn't he see that neither of them was interested?

A dog ran towards them, its owner a tiny figure by the harbour wall. It ran excitedly between their legs, leaping up to leave dirty paw marks on Norman's coat before turning to Vincent who said 'Good boy, good boy' and tried to kick it.

'Same with animals,' Norman said as the dog ran off to urinate in an untidy fountain over the sea wall.

'You can come out here some days and not see a soul from one end of the Prom to the other,' he continued. 'Some people don't know what they're missing.'

'The wind and the cold,' murmured Vincent.

But Norman didn't hear; he was too busy taking deep breaths of the cold sea air.

Led by Vincent and Derek, the three men walked towards the harbour, passing the dog's owner, her desperation turning to anger as the dog moved even further away.

'He's right up the other end, love,' said Norman; then turning to the others: 'She'll have to move a bit faster than that if she wants to catch him this side of Christmas.'

All three laughed.

Christmas was only three days away.

He pushed between them, pointing to the upturned boats and sacks of hanging mussels staked around the harbour. In the shelter of the harbour steps, the tarpaulin cover of a pile of deck chairs had blown loose, flapping rhythmically up and down like the skirt of a dancer, flashing stripes of red, yellow and blue canvas.

'Needs seeing to, that,' Norman said, and descended the stone steps to fasten the loose rope.

Derek and Vincent, determined not to be drawn in his wake, waited together at the head of the steps beside a blackboard forecasting more strong winds, and a torn flag flapping its warning to an empty sea.

'There must be a quicker way home than back along the Prom,' Derek said.

Vincent stamped his feet and moved to the shelter of a kiosk.

Derek read the inscription on a large wartime mine, mounted in concrete and rusted through its scarlet paint.

Beneath them Norman struggled with the rope. Both men watched. He waved to them and shouted that everything was under control but his forced laugh suggested otherwise and they saw the wind pull the rope from his hands.

'I don't know why he keeps going on about Alice,' Vincent said as Derek joined him beside the deserted kiosk. Both men smoked without removing their hands from their pockets.

'Alice? I hadn't really noticed.'

'He's always on about her, always putting her down.'

Derek was uncertain whether or not he should answer. 'You close, then, you and Alice?' he asked.

'Close? Yes, I suppose we are. We don't see much of each other, mind. I live in the Midlands . . .'

'Oh. Nice. What part?'

'Wolverhampton.'

'Oh, Wolverhampton . . .'

Both men turned away as their conversation petered out, stamping their feet against the cold, and impatient as Norman continued to struggle with the flapping tarpaulin.

'He's always doing things like that,' Vincent said. 'Always the Good Citizen bit.'

'Comes from being a policeman, I suppose.'

'Suppose so.'

They continued to watch, content to have made their excuses for Norman who, stepping back from the chairs, gave a final tug on the rope, clapped his hands free of dirt, and ran towards them, coming up the steps two at a time.

'Still fitter than most men half my age,' Vincent mimicked quietly as they trod out their cigarettes and walked to meet him.

'There. That should hold it secure. Some people couldn't tie a knot to save their lives.' He coughed and stood to catch his breath, going through the motions of brushing sand from his coat to hide his breathlessness. 'Not as . . . as young as I used to be. Mind you, I . . . I look after myself – have to in my line of work. Still fitter than many a man ten years younger.'

They turned away from him in the direction of home. Above the sea blinked the red and green lights of an aircraft. All three watched, searching for its outline.

'Most likely down from the aerodrome at Hundale,' Norman said. 'Some sort of trainer, most likely. Single engine, twin seater.' Now he stood alone and watched the lights, as though waiting to confirm his guess.

From looking at the cooked meats display in a neighbouring store, Rita studied the colourful designs pinned to the hardboard display of the town's only surviving tattoo parlour.

'Come Inside. No Obligation. Painless. Safe. Any Design.' The lettering was done in red on yellow along the narrow width of the shop front. Squeezed between the food store and a Cut Price Off Licence offering Irresistible Xmas Bargains, the tattoo parlour evoked a less hygienic, if somewhat more colourful past.

Rita was shopping for a small gift for Alice, an idea which had occurred to her the previous evening. Now, it had started to rain lightly and she sheltered beneath the canvas awning of the shop.

In the cooked meat display, pride of place went to a whole ham, coated with yellow breadcrumbs, a single pink slice cut from it and displayed alongside. At the far end of the window stood a four-tiered wedding cake, coated in pink and white and topped by tiny figures.

Next door the hardboard fascia of the tattoo parlour was covered in dragons, naked women, swords, ships, names, skulls, tigers and fish. There were names and scrolls for as little as five pounds, right up to a leaping tiger with oriental lettering for almost a hundred. It would be a brave man, she thought, who would trust a firm young body to the leaping tiger, prepared to spend a lifetime watching it dissolve with age and come apart with fat.

As she watched, the door opened and the tattooist himself appeared in the doorway, one step down from the level of the street. He saw Rita and winked before turning away to attempt the more serious business of lighting a cigarette in the wind. Despite the low temperature he only wore a string vest, and above the belt his body was almost entirely covered with tattoos. Swallows circled his neck, chased by a rattlesnake which struck from between his shoulder blades. He shivered and rubbed his arms. Where his own skin showed through, she saw that he was abnormally pale. He turned and saw her looking.

'Like it, do you, love? Keeps the cold out.' He laughed.

'Oh, no, I . . .'

'I look upon it as a form of advertising – a human sandwich-board.' He laughed at the joke he had told a thousand times, turning slowly and pointing over his shoulder at the designs on his back. People walked by with umbrellas. Rita felt embarrassed, trapped by the rain and the talking man.

Across his chest a dragon breathed fire, and his mother and Leeds United jockeyed for space across his muscular forearm.

'Colour 'em up now and again so as the punters can see what they look like. In the flesh, you might say.' Neither of them laughed at the joke. He went on: 'Not much doing this time of year – brisk enough during the season, mind, but not in this weather.' Rita looked back to the ham and then across to the wedding cake.

Over the man's heavy stomach a woman with yellow hair had bloated to Buddha-like proportions, her arms and legs flexing as he scratched at an elastoplast stuck between his nipples.

Behind him she could see a dark room, more colourful designs and a large mirror with the word 'Durex' printed across it. She looked away. The man continued talking, smoke accompanying each word.

'Getting to be popular with women, these days. Oh, yes. Flowers, butterflies. You'd be surprised at some of the places I've put a rosebud.'

In the neighbouring window a hair-netted shop assistant reached with tongs towards a tray of cakes. When she looked up the man grinned and waved. The girl pulled a face and withdrew.

'Been wanting me out of here for ten years,' he said proudly. 'Unhygienic. Wanted to condemn the property at one time.'

Rita looked up at the crumbling stucco of the two empty floors above the shop. The building condemned itself.

'Big row in the papers a few years back: one lot wanted me out and some others, local history or something, wanted to preserve the shop. Architectural interest. Not many of these old shops left, you see. Built a few hundred years since.' He looked proudly up at his decrepit property and at the newer, safer shops on either side. As he turned, the bluebirds on his neck stretched and shrank as though trying to escape.

'Not local yourself, then?'

'No. I—'

'Thought not. You can usually tell. Not much to do out of season, but everybody tries to look busy.'

As he spoke, a man crossed the road towards them, stopping in the middle and shouting at the traffic. As he approached, Rita recognised Devlin. Arriving beside them he pulled up his sleeve to reveal a small scroll and the word 'Mother'. The tattoo was recent, and around its edges grew a ring of scabs. The tattooist felt them, gathering the coloured skin between his finger and thumb. He told Devlin there was nothing to worry about: they'd be gone in a week. After this the two men stood without speaking, Devlin studying the board of designs.

'I could do you a snake, a nice cobra, three colours, for a tenner.'

Devlin stepped back from the window, mumbling something noncommital.

'What's wrong?' the man laughed. 'Not frightened, are you?' Rita saw the flash of hatred in Devlin's eyes before he laughed too and then pretended to punch the man in the stomach.

'If you don't fancy snakes how about a dagger? Very popular, daggers. Do more daggers than all the rest put together. Death's

136

heads are very—' The man broke off suddenly. 'We were all sorry to hear about your mother. It came as a bit of a shock.'

'Yes, well, can't grumble,' Devlin said. 'She had a good innings, nearly—' He stopped, uncertain of his mother's age, of what his ignorance might suggest.

'Aye, well,' the tattooist repeated, 'she's at rest now, God rest her soul. When's the, er . . .?'

'Day before yesterday. Crematorium.'

'Oh, aye, well, you've got yourself to see to now. Can't go on living in the past, can we?'

Devlin shook his head, gave the man another playful punch, and looked up and down the wet street as though expecting to see someone.

The tattooist said something and turned away. The two men touched each other on the shoulder and parted.

'Lost his mother,' the man said, as Devlin turned the corner. 'You might have heard about it. Died in a fire. Burned to death in a chalet out on the lighthouse road. Death traps, they are. Should have been pulled down years ago.' He pointed in the general direction of the lighthouse. Rita turned to look in the opposite direction, but Devlin was no longer in sight. She rubbed her chin and wiped the rain from her forehead.

'Buried her day before yesterday. Crematorium.' The discrepancy never occurred to him. 'He came in here a week since for her name doing on his arm. It's a nice job but the skin's still not settled. Nice, that, I thought. You won't get many sons coming in for something like that so soon after.'

Rita said 'No,' and the man turned and went into his shop, pausing only to throw his cigarette onto the wet pavement.

7

In the room off the warehouse, Morgan climbed a recently compacted cardboard bale and sat beside the girl who held his cup. The girl, no more than seventeen, wore a green nylon smock and had her hair flattened beneath a net. She worked in the butchery department, where it was her job to take out trolleys of butchered meat to the fridges, to scrub the steel and wooden surfaces and to sweep the sawdust floor. There were splashes of blood on her smock, brown and red, smudged where she had wiped at them. Struggling out of adolescence, she remained ugly, especially when compared with the older check-out assistants with their permed hair and painted nails. At one side of the girl's mouth was a patch of acne covered with pink powder.

She handed Morgan his plastic cup. Tea in his, oxtail soup with a white froth in hers. Sitting together, surrounded by the precarious piles of cardboard and knee-deep in polythene and paper, Morgan appeared the taller of the two.

Like Morgan, the girl spent most of her breaks and lunch hours away from the canteen. The previous day the two of them had sat on a wall behind the supermarket where it backed on to the town's only cinema. She had told him about the smell from the bins during summer and that she had worked at the store during the school holidays. She said she was lucky to have a full-time job there. Morgan had said 'Congratulations', and the girl had smiled.

Now, as she drank, Morgan was looking at her, at her mouth. She touched her spots self-consciously and asked him about the primitive baling machine, saying she supposed he had to be strong, flattering him as she tried to divert his attention from her face.

'Some of the women seen the panto,' she said. 'Good, they said. Said they enjoyed it. Took their kids.' She waited for him to answer. He didn't, and so she resumed talking. 'Said it's the best they've had in years. Most of 'em have lived here all their lives. Mona – that's the one with the funny eye – she only lives two doors away from us. She's got four kids. They've all been.'

Morgan picked a piece of black from the surface of his drink and flicked it into the room.

'Summer, they sometimes have discos and bands.'

Despite the season, three sluggish flies, kept warm and fat on the damaged packets of food, circled the high ceiling, weaving in and out and knocking clumsily against the fluorescent light. Morgan looked up to watch them and the girl said something about the device they had for killing them in the butchery room: a blue flashing light in a wire cage.

Morgan drank half his tea and threw the remainder over the cardboard at his feet.

The girl remembered something, touching his arm in her eagerness to tell him.

'Police was here. Up in Mr Williams's office. Two of 'em. I was up there for the order book. One of 'em said he knew you and asked how you was doing.' She spoke excitedly and Morgan half turned to listen.

'And?'

'They wanted him to put a picture up of that missing girl. But Mr Williams said it wasn't the sort of thing he wanted to have stuck up – not with it being so close to Christmas and all. He said' – and here she slowed down as she repeated the store manager's exact words – 'that a supermarket was not the proper place to display information of that sort. Told 'em straight. Not that they seemed to bother. They had this picture, photo of the missing girl. In the end he said he'd put it up in the loading bay so as the drivers could have a look at it. He said that if—'

'What did he look like, the copper?'

'Oh, well, one was a tallish fattish bloke and the other wasn't very old, nineteen or twenty, with a helmet. The fatter one was a sergeant with a cap. He was the one who had the picture.'

Morgan had never thought of Norman as being fat, but he supposed that to the girl anything over nine or ten stones would qualify.

Looking into her cup, the girl complained that it didn't taste much like oxtail. He said it looked like diarrhoea. She giggled and threw what was left against the opposite wall, where it splashed in a long line and ran down to the floor.

'Shit,' she said, and giggled again, disappointed when he didn't say anything. The three flies flew to investigate.

139

'How come he knows you, then, this copper? Not done anything have you?' She spoke more confidently now, as if about to reveal secrets of her own.

Morgan nodded, and said 'Murder'.

The girl said 'What!' and then began to laugh as she realised he was joking. For different reasons, Morgan laughed with her. She offered him a cigarette and they sat together, filling the windowless room with smoke. She asked him if Morgan was his real name and if he minded being so small, as though there had been an element of choice involved. He turned to stare at her and said that it suited him just fine. Then he pointed to her spots and asked her if she minded having a face like a dog's arse.

After a long silence in which neither of them spoke, the girl told him that she was able to get staff discount through her friend at Wines and Spirits . . . so if he ever wanted to buy anything cheap, cigarettes, things like that . . . He looked down and saw her legs, her clumsy shoes hanging beside his own.

As they sat without speaking, one of the butchers put his head round the door, whistled, and made a gesture to Morgan with his bended arm and fist.

When he'd gone the girl explained that he was the head butcher and that it was best not to say anything or answer back. 'It's all they ever talk about in there. You'd think that seeing all them bodies and things would put them off.'

'Bodies?'

'All the pigs and things.'

A bell sounded, and over the Tannoy a voice announced that the first dinner break had ended.

From her pocket the girl took a small mirror and a tube of cream. This she applied to the side of her mouth, where the white lotion remained more conspicuous than the spots. She pursed her lips at the results, studying her teeth in the mirror.

'What do you think?' She stood in front of him, her face several inches below his own.

'Invisible,' he lied, waiting for her to leave the room before he too slid to the ground. He heard the shouts of the other women as they returned to work. Slamming the door, he threw an empty box at the circling flies. The smell of the girl's lotion filled the room.

That night, midnight, it began to snow for the first time that winter. First time snow, settling on the cold ground. There was no accompanying wind, only a stillness through which the flakes fell and settled undisturbed. Only the club-shaped padding of a stray dog broke the whiteness, and cars left their treads like discarded snakeskins. The fields turned white and then the town. Only the sea shook off the snow.

In the morning, everyone would marvel at the whiteness and comment on how expected or unexpected it had been, how nice it looked, all white, and how quickly it would turn to dirty water, stained with the heat of the passing day.

A white Christmas, some said. But it wouldn't be: Christmas Day would be bright and sharp, pale blue sky, cold sun, the smell of cooking and sherry and dark early.

Through the night the snow fell against drawn curtains and warm chimneys. In the churchyards and cemeteries it coated the Dead, and in the allotments it drew a first shroud over Tracey Morton. Undisturbed, it covered her protruding feet, building on her coldness and collecting in a scree against the mound beneath which she lay.

The woman lay on the bed, naked, an inviting round shadow between her legs, her white buttocks clenching and relaxing. On the floor lay her nurse's uniform. She turned her head and moaned, her lips opening and closing like a fish. A clock on the wall said ten past four, and by the door stood a bearded doctor, white-coated, with a stethoscope in his hand. His frame filled the screen, cutting from front to rear view as he approached the woman.

In summer, the Palace Cinema catered to families sheltering from the rain, from the expense of the world outside or from the mid-week boredom of their holidays: James Bond films, Space Adventure and Walt Disney, week after week.

Now, the cinema was cold and smelled of mice. The jerkiness of the film pointed to where the more explicit scenes had been cut. In a room designed to hold three hundred sat an audience of forty, one of whom was Devlin. Watching the film, he remembered other occasions he had been here – times when he needed to bridge the inconvenient gap between matinées and evening performances, during which he stayed in the town instead of making the journey home to his mother.

The nurse on the bed had turned on to her stomach, backside

raised, legs open, arms outstretched and clinging to the metal bars of the bed. The doctor held his stethoscope to one heavy breast and she squealed unconvincingly.

Roland Trotter, also staying in town between the two shows (in his case to avoid the demands of his wife and children), had invited Devlin for a drink. Devlin had declined, offering his mother's recent death as an excuse where previously he would have offered none.

In the darkness of the cinema Devlin smiled at the success, so far, of his deception, at the false grief and the sympathy with which he continued to be surrounded. A schoolteacher had once told him that he had a good brain, if only he'd use it to better himself instead of . . . instead of . . . The man had thrown up his hands and told him to go.

The second film was delayed, and when it arrived was disappointingly and distractingly sub-titled.

During the interval the screen filled with the psychedelic patterns of moving oil.

The night before, Devlin had thought seriously about returning to the girl's body. But there had been too much risk involved. Besides which, he was uncertain what would remain of the body, or what would happen to it if he tried to move it.

He had passed the untidy hawthorn hedge bordering the allotments on several occasions, seeing the columns of dirty smoke and the men who still dug over the empty plots. He had realised then, and for the first time, that he didn't know precisely where the girl's body lay. This, more than anything else, made him uneasy, made him feel as though he had in some way lost control over what he had done, what was happening to him, what might happen if the body was found. But, he then argued, perhaps it was for the best that he didn't know for certain. Cranks never located bodies. Likewise innocent suspects. Only the murderers knew the exact location. So perhaps not knowing exactly where the body lay was a blessing in disguise, the one slender thread which might either connect and condemn him, or which might snap and absolve him of any involvement or responsibility for what had happened. No, he was certain he did not know the precise location of the body. How could he? So even a detailed confession would be useless. But would it? He knew the general whereabouts, and with dogs they were certain to turn something up.

Sitting in the unheated cinema, his confidence began to ebb away. It was a weakness, and if he had been able to identify it, others would too.

And then the lights dimmed and he felt safe again.

Beside the theatre car park stood a line of painted horses, the colour peeling from their dappled bodies. Alongside, like giant woodlice, stood a row of upturned boats, their wooden hulls bleached grey, taken for the winter from the boating pond, full now of sand and litter. The first snow had been quickly dispersed, leaving only strips of water over which ice formed each evening.

In parts, the fibre-glass bodies of the abandoned horses had been punctured, revealing their wire frames and hollow innards. Above them the gulls hung like buzzards waiting for a death. Sand blew across the open forecourt, collecting against the stone steps which sank into the beach. A man, bent against the wind, one hand on his head, crossed the tarmac to his car. He was a fat man, made fatter by his billowing coat. In the car he studied his face in the mirror, removing his hat and smoothing his hair before driving away.

Rita watched him, recognising him and his car. She stood in the doorway of a store where a downrush of warm air blew over her, sharing the space with two other women.

In the summer, a photographer and his miniature, red-jacketed monkey stood at the head of the steps. Children queued uncertainly to have the animal positioned on their shoulders, its serrated teeth chattering beside their ears and necks. At the photographer's feet stood a small wickerwork cage, slices of apple browning in its weave.

Beside Rita, in the window of a tobacconist's, hung plastic wallets of picture postcards. 'I can't find My Little Willie.' A string of fat, swim-suited women licking ice creams. A thousand different Capo di Monte molten men, women and children, unsold, unsellable now until the new season. Glass cats, horse brasses; plastic drunks with a hidden hole beneath their caps – 'Weepy Wee Wee: Top up with Water and Squeeze.' The man pisses against a lamp post. 'Very Popular,' the sign says. 'A Great Novelty.'

The women moved away. The car park was empty now. Behind her the door opened and Rita, too, moved off into the street.

BABY JESUS. THREE WISE MEN. THREE SHEPHERDS. Small white cards were printed with the names of those present at the birth. Alice read each one and looked at the corresponding figures, most of them hidden by the stiff straw spread across the floor of the wooden crib. FIGURES MADE BY the Children of Bellfield Primary School, AGES 5 – 7. The plaque hung above the roofline of the crib like the sign outside a pub. Among the figures, some plastic, others stuffed or wooden, stood small animals, sheep, cattle, pigs and a zebra. THE BABY JESUS, with upraised arms and legs, dwarfed them all, twice the size of its parents and dominating the stable. THE BABY JESUS, born in BETHLEHEM. MARY and JOSEPH, His Parents. Each of the kings wore a crown of gold and silver paper, their black and scarlet robes partially buried in the straw.

The glass-fronted display case in which the scene was set stood outside Boots the Chemist, four poles and a rope surrounding it. Beside it was a large wooden box in which Contributions were Gratefully Received.

'Grand. Our Margaret has a little girl at Bellfield – our Susan. Look how they've put the little clothes on.'

'Yes, lovely,' said Alice to the woman now standing beside her.

'They generally reckon to get something up on a Christmas time. Last year they had a show, a play thing. Our Susan was an angel. Her mother made these coathanger things for her wings. Always been good with her hands, our Margaret. She's got a photograph somewhere.'

Alice was suddenly conscious of standing between the woman and her granddaughter's achievement. She stood to one side.

'Thanks, love.' The woman had been waiting for her to move.

At the back corner of the stable lay the origami star of Bethlehem, where it had fallen from its wire announcing the miraculous birth.

'Got any grandchildren of your own, have you?' the woman asked.

'Two,' said Alice without stopping to think. The answer came more easily and seemed more natural than the truth. 'Boy and a girl. Nine and seven.'

'Mmm, nice. Boy and a girl.'

'Nine and seven. Bit of a handful, mind. David and Wendy.'
The names also came without thinking, as though they had been
there all the time, ready to support her lie.

'Mmm, nice.'

'David and Wendy,' Alice repeated, smiling to herself as the
woman moved closer to the glass case to study the efforts of her
own solitary grandchild. She read the cards aloud, guessing at
the contribution made by her granddaughter. The shepherds?
The crib? The BABY JESUS himself? Fancy that! The BABY
JESUS himself!

Two days before Christmas, Vincent announced that Mr Berryman had offered him a flat in his own large house. He had
accepted, and intended moving in during the first week in
January.

Derek said, 'Well done.' Norman tried to decide on the best
thing to say (and consequently said nothing until later), and
Morgan said, 'Good riddance.' Alice hid her disappointment,
and she, too, congratulated her brother. It was obvious from the
way Vincent made the announcement that he considered the
move to be a good one, and that congratulations were in order.
Rita kissed him on the cheek and predicted that before long he
would be a millionaire. Mr Berryman had apparently hinted at
some kind of promotion and had elaborate plans for Vincent's
future. Norman said that he thought Morgan's remark a little
uncharitable. Morgan said he'd been joking, and held out his
small hand for Vincent to shake. Everyone watched and, with
that one gesture, they were all convinced that for Vincent at least
Better Things lay ahead.

That evening Alice took out the bottle of wine she had bought
for their Christmas lunch, and Norman, as was his custom every
Christmas, read the label with an exaggerated German accent,
drew out the cork, sniffed it and pronounced the year a good
one. Alice, by a series of nods and knowing looks, ensured that
no one interrupted the ritual. They drank to Vincent.

'We've set him on the Right Path,' Norman said later as they
lay in bed. 'We've given him a Good Start.'

For his sake, she did not argue. 'Luck,' she thought to herself.
It was all down to luck. And when Norman was asleep she cried
briefly at the thought of losing her brother.

In his room, Vincent tore up Maureen's solitary letter, all

serious thoughts of a reconciliation long since abandoned.

The following morning Norman offered his own hand to be shaken. Alice looked on. The scene reminded her of the happy ending of a film. This time she made no attempt to hide her tears, and Norman indicated to Vincent that the privilege of comforting her was his. After a few seconds Alice pushed him off and waved them both away from her, declaring that she was behaving like a silly child. Norman and Vincent shared their first glance of genuine understanding. Laughing, they agreed with her and, not long after, Norman left for work, leaving Alice and her brother alone.

She now gave him bedding, crockery, cutlery, and, from one of the empty bedrooms, an electric kettle. She kissed him and said again how happy she was for him.

That same evening Derek and Veronica arrived with a porcelain tile upon which 'Vincent's Room' was painted ('Hand-painted,' Derek said), and Rita with another bottle of wine, which she presented to Norman to open. This time the accent was what he supposed to be Bulgarian. The first glass was ceremoniously passed to Vincent to taste, and another toast was drunk.

After the meal Norman made a little speech, confessing to them all that as a part of the search for the missing girl a file had been composed of all likely suspects, known criminals and new or unfamiliar characters in the town and that, upon his arrival, Vincent's name had been added to the list.

'By you, Norm?' Vincent asked. It was the one question Norman had hoped to avoid. 'Not that I blame you, Norm. Only natural.'

Norman had wanted to explain the moral conflict and standards of professional behaviour involved, but he simply nodded contritely and said 'Thank you'.

'He didn't even arrive until after the kiddy had gone missing,' Alice said.

'It's all right, Alice; he was only doing his job. Right, Norm?' Norman nodded and looked around the table, determined to respond correctly to his brother-in-law's magnanimity.

Morgan asked if any more of them were on the list. Norman said he wasn't sure, and before anyone could say anything to spoil the occasion, Alice announced that they were all being silly. Everyone agreed with her, and Norman presented Vincent with a pair of cuff links, which made Alice want to cry again.

'Cheers, Norm. Cheers.'

'Lovely.'

'Mm, nice.'

'Class, that. Not too flashy.'

Vincent held them against his wrist and tried to think which, if any, of his shirts had the necessary holes.

Two hundred yards from the theatre stood an empty building in which shows had also once been held, but which was now used only as a store for the larger pieces of scenery and stage equipment.

On warm days Devlin wheeled pieces of exotic jungle and fairy-tale castles between the two buildings, pausing reluctantly for fathers to pose their children and take photographs. The building, like the theatre, overlooked the sea and the expanse of level sand to the south of the town. The tourists ventured this far only to hack at the immature mussels which coated the groynes like bubbling tar.

Before reaching the store – known as the Old Theatre by many of the older locals – the Promenade turned sharply inland. Beyond the turn stretched a golf course, a line of bungalows and, beyond those, the start of the south shore caravan parks. People walked as far as the old theatre and turned back towards the town, spread out before them on warm summer nights in beads of yellow and blue, vibrant with the sound of fairgrounds and the smell of frying food and beer.

On the roof of the old theatre stood a dome from which all the glass had fallen. A notice nailed to the door of the staircase warned that the tower was unsafe.

Through the empty frames, Devlin looked out over the town.

In 1941, an off-course German raider had dropped a string of bombs, killing sixteen, injuring over a hundred people and demolishing forty-two homes. One of the bombs had fallen near the old theatre and had started a fire as a result of which much of the original building had to be destroyed. People still remembered the war and the bombs, and the softened outline of one crater still served as a bunker on the golf course.

Devlin looked down at the traffic and at the solitary walkers on the beach, at the rows of houses and the railway lines bending in and out of the town in a giant S. Looking out like that, seeing the boundaries of the town, made him realise for the first time how small a place it really was.

Out towards the lighthouse he saw the string of black chalets lining the distant road. He counted along to where his own home had been. This made him think of his mother and he imagined her looking out towards the broken outline of the dome in which he now stood. She, too, had remembered the old theatre.

On a ledge below him, he saw a line of pigeons, pressed together against the cold. He spat down at them, missing, but unsettling them with the noise. He grinned as they moved nervously apart, falling and flying into the drag of the wind.

8

Norman sat in his makeshift shelter at the centre of the allotments, his own black and desolate plot around him, his feet resting on a yard-high pile of *Police Gazettes*. In the corner of the shed sat another, older man, in wellingtons and a gaberdine overcoat tied with string. He smoked an inch of slender cigarette without removing it from his mouth. Norman waved at the smoke between them, but he seemed not to notice.

Picking up a magazine, Norman displayed the centre pages for the man to see. A line of five policewomen in tightly belted tunics and wearing fishnet stockings high-kicked in chorus. The women all wore scarlet lipstick and pursed their lips in the direction of the camera. Their skirts were not of regulation length and they all displayed a few inches of leg above their stockings.

'Harmony singers, or some such,' Norman said, using the old-fashioned term for the chorus. 'Local division. Play at all the local police functions, charity concerts, that sort of thing.' There was a note of contempt in his voice. 'The one in the middle's a sergeant. You wouldn't think it to look at her, would you? "Police Five" they call themselves. That's a joke.' He laughed coldly and waited for the man to speak.

He said, 'Aye,' because that was all that was required of him and then he too began to laugh. This gathered itself into a drawn out spasm of coughing.

Norman waited in silence, flinching as a ball of phlegm shot through the open door.

The high-kicking policewomen were the nearest the gazette ever came to frivolity. This was the Christmas issue. The rest of its glossy pages were filled with articles on police work, commendations, dogs with their handlers and motor-cycle riders formed into impressive pyramids.

It was Christmas Eve, and since the previous evening Norman had been on holiday, not due to return until the morning of the twenty-eighth – his longest Christmas break in six years (as he had pointed out to everyone at home, and as he now told the man sitting opposite him).

Something irritated Norman about the policewomen and the sergeant at their centre. Almost fifteen years his junior, and brazen enough to . . . He kept his thoughts to himself.

After a long silence he said something about the weather and the condition of the soil. The old man cleared his throat to speak, but Norman interrupted him: 'They all think everything stops at Christmas,' he said. 'They simply don't realise what's happening, here, now, under this very ground.' He banged his foot on the floor of his shed and smiled to himself, constantly amazed by the miracle of growth of great sunflowers from striped seeds the size of a fingernail, of row after row of caterpillar-pocked cabbages from nothing. To the old man it seemed less of a miracle and he listened without enthusiasm.

'I was trying to explain it to our lodgers – we keep a guest house, see – well, the wife, really – anyhow, I was trying to explain what it is about the soil, what it takes before you can begin to grow anything, before you get any return on your effort . . .'

The old man got up and thanked him for the tea. Not wanting to detain him, Norman rose too. Neither of them was able to stand upright in the cramped space.

From the doorway Norman looked along the line of the abandoned railway; from there across the half-built housing estate, over the cemetery and into the town itself. He breathed deeply, thumping his chest and blowing warm shapes into the cold air. The rhythmic sound of earth being chopped at attracted his attention and he turned to watch as the old man forced his fork into the hard ground, turning it black from the white of the fading frost.

Three days of holiday ahead, four including Christmas, Christmas Day tomorrow and a whole morning to himself on the allotment.

Returning to his shed he looked again at the photograph of the five policewomen in their fishnet stockings. He looked closely at the sergeant, at her young features and dark, smiling lips. 'Five Girls Set for Success' the article was headed, going on to say that a successful career as recording or cabaret artistes awaited the women should they ever wish to leave the force – a move all of them strenuously denied ever wanting to make; police work was their life and all hoped for further promotion within the force. The writer of the article said that he was sure they would all get to where they wanted to be, and that they had the best wishes and full support of all the local forces. It was then that Norman realised that the woman (whom he had never met) reminded him of Veronica, that she looked too much like an entertainer for him ever to be able to take her seriously as a policewoman – too heavily painted, too keen on display, too self-centred, just like Veronica. He imagined her *as* Veronica, dancing and singing and kicking her legs, showing them off to other policemen, to other men, who shouted and whistled. Or was he thinking of Rita?

He threw the gazette to the floor without trying to understand the violence of his reaction. Even here the distant sound of chopping earth reached him. Beyond it he could hear a church bell, followed by the ten peals of a clock. He checked his watch and went outside to look once again over the town, out over the calm sea, and down the gently curving coast where dark smudges indicated other towns and villages, and where the caravan camps stood out as colourful flecks. He tested the air for wind, but there was none. He listened for the sounds of the town, but heard nothing.

A few minutes later the silence was broken by a shout from the old man. Norman looked up and silently cursed, impatient to begin his own morning's work. The man raised his fork into the air and pointed from it to the mound of compost at his feet. Norman wanted to shout back and ask him if he knew how much his holidays meant to him and how much he'd been looking forward to an uninterrupted day alone. People expected too much of him. The man dropped his fork and took several paces backwards. Norman sighed. They always expected too much.

Christmas Eve

'Midnight. Danes Head coastguard,' the man said and pointed to the flare.

His young partner continued to clap and blow into his gloved hands. They stood beside their car, each leaning over an open door and watching the falling ball of light, closing their eyes and seeing its path of descent etched across their eyelids. The powerful lights above the site of the girl's body still shone over the allotments – a white, cold light in a freezing night.

'They fire it every Christmas Eve at midnight. Wait a sec and you'll hear the bells.'

But the man wasn't listening. Already he was back in his seat and rubbing condensation from the windscreen. The distant pealing began, rising to a crescendo before fading to a reverberating silence.

'Any ideas who did it, have they?' The younger constable took his place in the car. He remembered the girl's mother in the market.

'A bit keen, aren't you, son?' The man laughed and said that it would soon wear off.

There was no body now and they guarded only the site in which a clue might lie – an eight by six foot enclosure in which the approximate shape of arms and legs lay staked out in white string.

'She'll be in Leeds by now,' the older man said. 'In the freezer until everybody gets back after Christmas.' The idea amused him and he laughed. The younger man laughed too, not because he thought it was funny but because he was new to the job and still learning by example.

'They'll be wanting to search the gardens.'

'The allotments? Aye, more than likely – though they've not much chance of turning anything up after all this time.'

'No, I suppose not.'

Bales of straw had been packed around the protective structure of wood and polythene, and heavy wooden planks had been laid as walkways across the trampled earth. The land surrounding the site had been marked with metal rods and rope from which hung coloured plastic tabs. At the entrance to the shelter a white cross announced No Unauthorized Admittance, its shadow stretching over the ground ahead of the powerful lights.

At six in the morning, Christmas Day, the two men would be relieved and others would come to take their place. They had been there since ten, two hours; they had heard the town below them as it sank noisily into the night. A slight wind tugged at the sheets of polythene covering the shelter, sucking them in and out, taut and slack, like a hidden drum beating a dirge through the night.

The faces of the two men were reflected in the glass of the windscreen, and they watched themselves as the descending flare swung slowly down into the sea.

'We had a ship go down this time last year. Caught on the banks out by The Head and then turned over. They got everybody off, but it still went down. Had a foreign firm in – Dutch, I think – to salvage it. You get things like that, living by the sea.'

'Yes, I suppose so.'

The men stared out, their conversation exhausted.

At half past midnight they drank tea and the older man filled the car with smoke.

'They'll put another one up in an hour.'

'Another?'

'Flare. A green one this time.'

'Oh.'

The time passed slowly, the fluorescent hand of the dashboard clock moving from second to second as they watched, staring back out into the darkness at nothing, ignoring the radio and humming occasionally to break the silence.

At one o'clock, the second flare rocketed, burst, rose in an arc, and then fell along the path of the first towards the sea. The older man looked at his watch and said 'One o'clock.' The dashboard clock said five to. An hour had passed.

'You don't hold out much hope, then? Finding her killer, I mean.'

'No hope for any of us, lad. No hope at all.' It was the kind of thing people said for effect, without thinking.

'Only fourteen, she was.'

'Fourteen, fifteen, sixteen. What difference does it make? But

I'll tell you something – if she'd been forty, then there wouldn't have been half the fuss. Not by a long chalk.'

The younger man looked surprised. Even the older man felt uneasy about what he had said, the way it had sounded.

'Well, perhaps not to that extent,' he added, nudging the younger man. 'We wouldn't be out here getting our arses frozen stiff for a start, would we?'

'No, I suppose not. But fourteen. What sort of bloke would do something like that to a fourteen-year-old child?'

'Listen, son. All kinds of people do all kinds of things to all kinds of others. You'll learn that soon enough if nothing else.'

The green flare continued to fall, drifting downwards like a tadpole through the darkness.

'They used to signal to incoming boats with flares about the tides and things,' the older man said several minutes after the flare had vanished. 'All done by radio now, though.'

The younger man looked out at the fragile structure covering the site where the body had been found and tried to imagine the outline of the girl beneath it. He listened to the older man and wondered if he too would become impervious to such events.

'Be a local man, you think?' he asked.

'What? This? No. Place's too small. Everybody knows every-body else.' The man said no more, unwilling, perhaps, to be proved wrong in the eyes of a novice.

There their conversation ended, neither of them wanting to take it any further.

An hour after the second flare, a third, phosphorous-white, burst and fell gracefully into the sea.

In the wake of each broken snore came the echo of a wheeze, an outrush of air which whistled faintly from the man's chest, dying in his mouth and wetting his lips. Occasionally he started, as though shocked by his dream.

The corridor light, left on by another tenant, shone through the glass panel at the top of the door. On a chair lay Rita's clothes. Beyond them, stretched upright in a glass case, stood the World's Smallest Man, his features invisible in the half light, dried and twisted.

Earlier, the Freak Show man had told her about a duck-billed platypus owned by his father, a perfectly natural animal, no deformities whatsoever, but which the holidaymakers had queued to see, suspended by wire, its glassy doll-eyes peering across a waterless riverbed in search of fish. Back in the thirties, that had been. Listening to him had reminded her of Norman, and she thought of him now, lying awake in the darkness, of him and Alice at home, together, waiting for Christmas.

At the centre of the room stood a table crowded with tins and bottles, some open, the smell of jellied meat and butter. On the floor lay a spilled ashtray. The man had apologised for the state of the room. She told him she had seen worse. It was the truth and he believed her.

'There he is,' he had announced proudly, turning on the light. 'World's Smallest Man.' His eyes were closed, his lips drawn tightly back in a half smile to reveal rows of tiny, pointed teeth. His entire head was no larger than Rita's fist. There were no branches or twigs in the case to suggest his real origins, only a yellow cigarette and an old penny as a measure of scale.

'One season I had him with the fag in his mouth,' the man said proudly. 'Smoking. Couldn't light it, of course.'

On the shelf beside the ape stood a shoe, a column of silver change and a large black spider entombed in a block of clear plastic. He invited her to touch it, to feel it.

Down one wall of the room stood an unmade bed, its blankets spilling on to the floor. The man began to fill the kettle, swearing as cold water splashed his hands. He lit a small gas fire and invited her to take off her coat.

Along the corridor a man and woman shouted at each other, and a baby cried. Rita turned to listen, looking up at the light above the door. On the floor beside her stood a saucepan half full of dirty water. She felt suddenly desolate, remembering the time, the date and the cold walk home ahead of her.

'Leaks,' the man said, indicating a rose-shaped stain on the ceiling.

Rita nodded and looked at the small man in his glass case.

'Shame about that platypus. Stuffing started to come out. Too warm, see. The old man kept it too warm. You have to keep things like that cool, otherwise . . .' He gave her a cigarette and sat beside her on the bed. Prising off his shoes, he complained at their tightness: they often did that, anything to distract from the fact that they were beginning to undress.

She wanted to suggest that they turn the glass case round or cover it up like a bird cage.

'Get the spiders from Hong Kong. Pound wholesale.' He spoke like a successful businessman who had just clinched a profitable deal. Gradually, however, his drunkenness returned. Forced deep by the cold night air, the long walk home and the promise of the woman on his arm, it surfaced to clip his sentences and pull at his eyelids. He dropped his cigarettes and swore as she knelt to pick them up.

Intermittently, in the darkness, she heard the baby cry and the woman's voice followed by the sound of something being dropped or thrown. She waited, eyes open, listening, feeling the weight of the man beside her in the narrow bed. His drunkenness had rendered him incapable, but sleep had saved him from embarrassment. He had forgotten to turn off the gas fire and it still burned with occasional popping sounds.

There were no decorations around the room, not even a card, only a calendar of a woman with a gun two years out of date. In the darkness Rita listened to his wheezing and moved her shoulder from under his chin. Despite the fire, the room was cold. On the floor lay his trousers and shirt, the sleeves outstretched across the linoleum floor.

Later, walking home, she passed a news-stand announcing the discovery of the missing girl. It didn't say if she was dead or not, but the word 'discovery' suggested the worst. She thought about the man, oblivious of her departure, and about the corpse staring across at him, the child waiting to share his Christmas. She thought, too, about Alice – about the present she had bought and wrapped, about the way Alice treated her and the confidences they had shared.

It was Christmas Day, but Rita didn't realise it. Nor did she see the second flare, green and vivid, as it sank beneath the sea to become a reflection of the moon.

Morgan lay on the bed and masturbated with Veronica Priestley dancing before his closed eyes. She wore the same tight tunic she had worn at the pantomime, but with the top drawn down to reveal her slumped white breasts and brown nipples, and with the crotch slit and drawn up to expose the shaking white skin of her thighs. He imagined himself on top of her, clasping himself to her waist and riding with her motions, his thick lips and wet tongue beneath her breasts as they swung on either side of his face. He heard her squeals of pleasure as he continued to move in and out of her, his feet joined around her buttocks. She was shouting his name, pressing him harder towards her, stroking the back of his head.

And as he masturbated, he intoned her name. Ve-ro-ni-ca, Ve-ro-ni-ca, Ve-ro-ni— feeling the warm liquid run over his closed fist.

Roland Trotter's oldest, fattest daughter was expecting a horse for Christmas. She raced along the carpeted hallway of their bungalow home slapping her cream jodhpured thighs, yelling 'Gee up' and, in a quieter voice, 'Good Boy,' and 'Snowy'. She wore a riding helmet and in the hallway hung a riding crop. Roland Trotter poured himself a second drink and pitied the horse, already paid for and awaiting collection in the morning.

His youngest daughter contented herself with a talking, wetting, eye-rolling doll which, he had calculated, cost roughly the equivalent of half a year's road tax or forty stall seats at a matinée. He was frequently given to such calculations.

It was almost midnight and despite his arguments about ten o'clock being a reasonable bedtime for a fourteen-year-old, especially on Christmas Eve, his wife had insisted that he was being old-fashioned and continued to indulge her children.

The room in which he stood was dominated by an oversized artificial tree, erected over a fortnight ago and drowning the room with its brilliance, flashing on and off and giving him a headache. He thought back to his own childhood Christmases, to the days before it had become such an expensive exercise and challenge: oranges, apples, nuts, shining threepenny pieces and silver sixpences. Once, there had even been a lump of coal (traditional, and for luck, his father had explained). He wondered what would happen if he gave his own daughter a lump of coal instead of a pony. Ordinarily, the thought would have amused him.

He looked out across his expensively maintained lawn where the gnomes fished in leaf-filled ponds, and where the lights of the town shone in a much duller display than those of his own open-plan living room and great silver tree. The line of red and yellow Japanese conifers skirting the drive looked more artificial than usual against the darkness.

Whilst fully aware of the need to remain conspicuously wealthy and successful, Roland couldn't help wondering if things weren't beginning to get out of hand, if there wasn't, perhaps, too great a difference between a shining threepenny bit (his father had unceremoniously burned the coal) and a galloping pony with braided mane and tail.

His thoughts were interrupted by his wife as she shouted for their children to give her a goodnight kiss. He, too, would be expected to bend down and kiss them. At his feet he felt the beribboned chihuahua which she also kissed. In the park he had seen a man throwing a rubber bone for a Great Dane to fetch. 'Nice dog,' he had said enviously, realising that the rubber bone was larger than the dog he was holding. 'Nice dog,' the man had replied, adding that he could hardly afford to feed it.

Roland tried to estimate how much Christmas had cost him, thinking of the cases of wines and spirits which lined the garage in preparation for the Boxing Day visit by relatives (invited by his wife to let them see how successful and happy they were).

Beyond his garden and the land bordering the golf course, he could make out the black squares of the chalets. The fire had unsettled him, and twice since he had dreamed of his own home burning down and of his wife and children screaming for him to jump, and then turning away to study a pile of presents salvaged from their hiding place and lined beside the road. He thought about the woman burned to death, and about her son.

His thoughts were rudely interrupted.

'Gee up! Whoa! Over the fence!'

He turned as his daughter raced around him, her whipping arm barely missing his legs. His wife watched smiling from the doorway, her frame filling the space.

'Just look at that,' she said affectionately, pointing to the girl, who continued to stampede around the furniture, trotting now like a Lipizzaner. 'She's a natural. Anyone can see that.'

Roland tried to look pleased.

'Who's going to be Mummy's little horsewoman of the year, then?'

The girl charged towards her, blowing a hunting horn, before turning towards the kitchen in search of a fox.

'You could at least show a little enthusiasm, give her some encouragement,' she said, coming into the room and lifting the glass from his hand to sniff into it and pull a face. 'Blood pressure,' she said, and stood sideways to view the reflection of her stomach in the picture window, running her ringed and braceleted hand over its sagging globe.

He watched her, remembering the Wakefield miner's daughter she had once been: bleached blonde hair, hourglass figure, pink slacks and stiletto heels.

'Nearly two pounds this week,' she said and waited for him to admire her.

'Svelte,' he said quietly.

'What?'

'Nothing. I just said "Well done".'

'Oh.'

Then she sat at one end of the long sofa and told him that it was the simple things which made Christmas special for her. He said he knew what she meant, and from somewhere came the taste of his first tangerine. Upstairs, his daughter hurdled over a linen basket and crashed to the floor.

He smiled. 'Four faults.'

'What?'

'Nothing. Just thinking.' He wanted to laugh.

'Coming to bed?' she asked.

'No, I thought I'd stay up and wait for the midnight flare. I like these local traditions. Only ten minutes.'

'Stupid if you ask me.'

'No one did,' he said bravely as the door slammed behind her. And turning to face the window, he looked out over the invisible sea and waited.

Veronica sat looking into the mirror. In the bed behind her she saw Derek, the eiderdown drawn to his chin, one exposed arm holding the thick paperback he had been reading for the previous month. She watched as he turned the pages, and thinking he might look across to where she sat, she resumed brushing her hair.

The extension of the pantomime into the New Year had given them all a boost, a promise of better things to come.

Veronica was almost forty-six, and she could see the years in her face. She still had a good head of hair – everyone commented on it – but there were rings around her eyes and lines beginning to spread from the corners of her mouth.

'Derek,' she said suddenly, watching him in the mirror, not really knowing why she had spoken or what she wanted to say.

'Mmm?' He turned another page, and looked up.

'What about after the pantomime, what then?'

'What do you mean? Same as usual, I suppose. Back down to the Midlands, my mother's, your father's, and into the agency to see what's going.' He lifted himself and turned to look at the reflection of her face, the book flat on his chest. 'Why?'

'Oh, nothing . . .'

Still watching her, he said, 'To tell you the truth, I fancy another shot at some cruise work . . . something on a ship, abroad. We'd make a fortune in Spain, places like that . . . Marbella . . . Benidorm.'

She saw him smile as he began to day-dream about what they might achieve.

'But those places want singers and comics and dancers. They don't want magicians. They want people who—'

'How do you know until you've tried?' He was angry at her refusal, even now, to share his optimism. 'Magicians are becoming much more popular . . . On the telly all the time. Everywhere you look these days . . .' But even he sounded unconvinced. 'People are getting tired of singers. They want something with a bit more novelty, something different. Let's face it, anybody can sing.'

'And tell jokes,' she added, agreeing with him because she was tired of fighting and because she wanted to believe him.

'Exactly. What people want is something with a bit more life. They want real entertainment. They can hear jokes any time, and they've only got to turn on the radio if it's singing they want.'

'I suppose you're right.'

'Of course I'm right. You'll see. Come August we'll be on a luxury liner anchored off . . . off the Canaries, the Scilly Isles. Select cabaret, proper tricks – none of this rabbit and cards stuff. Mysticism, that's what people want. Decent stuff – illusions, hypnotism – they're the big earners.' He looked from her reflection to his own. 'A bit of class.' He lifted his chin and stared at himself.

'No more kids' functions, then?'

He laughed. 'Kids' functions? Rubbish! Bread and butter money – that's all they've ever been – something to tide us over slack periods, that's all.'

As she listened, she found herself believing him, wanting to believe him. 'Come spring, I'll lose a bit of weight,' she said to herself, sitting upright and smoothing the dressing gown down over her waist.

' 'Course you will. Come spring everything will buck up.' He watched her, watched her hands feel over her body, saw her loose hair fall in a rope over her shoulder, saw her eyes looking from her own reflection to his.

'I've been meaning to knock the kids' stuff on the head for a long time,' he said quietly. 'We'll see out the pantomime and then start to build up something a bit better, something more refined.' He stopped and she saw him smile.

'What about the rabbits?' she asked suddenly, remembering them in their cramped baskets in the dark corridor.

'Rabbits?' The question surprised him. 'Oh, the rabbits! We'll have no time for rabbits if—'

'No, I mean now. What about the rabbits over Christmas? Who's looking after them until we get back?' She turned from the mirror to face him. 'Who's going to feed them?'

'Forget the f— forget the rabbits. That's all been taken care of.' Now she knew he was lying. 'The caretaker said he'd be in to look after them.'

'Oh.' She turned back to the mirror. Behind her, he began to list the programme they would offer, the places they would perform.

'And all free of charge,' he said. 'Halfway round the world and not a penny spent.'

'We'd even be paid for doing it,' she said, looking down and pulling the hairs from her brush.

'And after a year we'd have enough for a deposit on a house.' Now he was throwing ropes from his dreams to hers. He waited for her response.

'A house?' She turned to face him, as if his reflection was a mask which could not be trusted, whose sincerity she could not believe. 'A house?'

'Nothing but. Somewhere nice and stylish. In the country, perhaps. Somewhere down south.'

She began to nod, wanting him to continue, adding details of her own.

As she spoke, moving from kitchen to dining room to garden, he watched her, saw her excitement. Perhaps he was wrong to encourage her. Perhaps it was better not to talk about the things they knew they had no hope of achieving.

'Veronica.'

She opened her eyes and saw him lift the sheets. She looked

down again at her body, feeling the weight of her stomach and her thighs as they pressed together. She felt suddenly cold and saw herself reflected in the window where the curtains refused to meet. The light went out, and in the darkness she walked quickly to the bed.

'You did mean it?' she said, touching his warm back and legs. 'You did mean it about packing in the kids' functions, about that much at least?'

Later, as she lay with her head on his arm, watching the grey shapes of the room around her and thinking of Christmases spent as a child before her mother's death, a dull red glow lit up the wall opposite the window. She turned to find its source, but as she did so it faded and disappeared. She waited for it to return, thinking about what he had said and watching him as he slept. As a child she had always made wishes on Christmas Eve.

Devlin sat alone in his rented room.

The man from the insurance company had seen him three days after the fire and had told him that there were things which needed to be sorted out and that he would contact him in the New Year. He commiserated with Devlin but from the way he had looked at him, Devlin knew that there was something wrong. They had stood together beside the small square of scorched ground, the meeting of black and grass remarkably straight. They had seen the occupants of the other chalets standing in their doorways discussing what had happened. On a neighbouring plot a new For Sale sign waited for the coming summer when new grass would have appeared. It had started to rain and the man had offered him a lift back into town.

The landlady had invited Devlin to spend Christmas Eve with her, her husband and their two other lodgers – both sailors, she said, home from the sea. Devlin told her he had other plans.

Now he heard them downstairs, heard her in and out of the kitchen and the knock of glass against glass and the cheer which greeted each new bottle and plate of food. The two sailors and her husband made the noise of a dozen men.

At regular intervals one of them would run upstairs to use the toilet opposite his room. Hearing them approach he would turn out his light and sit in the darkness. Only when the living room door slammed behind them did he put the light back on. That single downstairs room seemed to hold the warmth of the entire house.

On his transistor radio he heard a choir singing carols, a military band and a woman speaking in a language he didn't understand. Beside him on the bed lay the newspaper in which the discovery of the girl's body was announced. He had read it and waited, expecting something to happen.

The landlady had mentioned the girl as he and the other men sat together at the table. 'Who could have done such a thing?' She shook her head. 'Animals,' one of the sailors had said. 'Want hanging. Worst thing they ever did, abolish hanging. Want to bring it back. Give them something to think about.' The other lodger and the woman's husband agreed with him.

Their unthinking references to the murderer as 'him' worried Devlin: already assumptions were being made which pointed – however vaguely – in the right direction. He asked them questions to see how much more they were prepared to assume, to guess at. The older of the two sailors asked Devlin if he had known the girl, and Devlin said that he had never heard of her. The men looked surprised, but continued eating, mopping the gravy off their plates and confidently predicting that the killer would be caught. Devlin agreed with them, adding to their list of suggested punishments, feeling secure in his condemnation of what had happened. The woman was the only one who seemed genuinely concerned, the men interested only in punishments and revenge. The sailors began to recount some of the things they had seen happen to criminals abroad, especially in the Middle East. Not seen, exactly, but things they had heard about from other sailors, things you wouldn't believe.

'Well, that's one family's Christmas down the drain,' the husband had announced.

Alone in his room, the announcement of the discovery worried Devlin far more than he had imagined it would. Tearing the small announcement from the paper he read it one last time, then tore it into tiny pieces, putting these inside a paper bag and that in the waste bin. An hour later he retrieved the bag and put it in his coat pocket. He was about to leave when the sound of the woman on the landing stopped him. He switched off his light. She knocked gently and tried the handle of his locked door. He waited until she had gone before daring to move. Then he took off his coat and stood by the window. Below him a group of drunks moved between the cars, singing the same few lines of a carol over and over.

Now, in the dark room, a victim of his own imagination, he thought about his mother and her death. He thought also of the time when, as a boy, he had first come to live by the sea. He tried to remember what he had been like as a child, but could not – his mind filled now only with what he had become.

The singers in the street continued their singing and from somewhere more distant came the sound of a bottle being smashed.

By early evening, news of the discovery had spread through the town. The second edition of the paper printed the item in the Stop Press column, which was otherwise empty.

At six, the light rain had turned briefly to sleet and then to snow which faded on the pavements.

'It's murder, Alice,' Norman said as they lay together in bed. 'It's definitely murder.' He couldn't keep the excitement out of his voice. 'Eight weeks the M.O. reckons. Eight weeks and—'

'M.O.?'

'Medical Officer. Doctor.' He sighed impatiently at her interruption. Surely she'd heard him talk about the M.O. before? Did that mean that she hadn't known what the initials stood for all this time? The thought left him reluctant to continue, but he was unable to resist going on.

'Eight weeks and not so much as an inkling.'

'It's going to make somebody look a bit of a fool, I daresay.'

'Not twenty feet from what?'

'Oh, nothing. What happens now, then?' Alice closed her eyes and let her head sink into the pillow, her head filled with thoughts of the following day.

Norman continued to stare up at the ceiling. His perverse sense of delight in the discovery had shocked her at first, but now she understood and accepted it. He had explained his role, his professional role in the proceedings, and then had confessed to his disappointment at not being recalled from leave after volunteering.

The officers at the allotments had been brought in from Leeds ('The three wise men,' one of his colleagues had called them). They had questioned him as though he was a civilian, suspicious, at first, of his calm and practised manner, of the fact that he appeared undisturbed by the discovery. They asked him for the precise time at which the body had been found. Not being able to tell them to the exact minute embarrassed him.

'Sergeant in the local force, eh?' one of the men had remarked sarcastically. He had heard them laughing and watched from his shed as they walked without thinking over soil beneath which seeds had been planted and were waiting to grow.

In words and phrases which lacked feeling and which distanced them all from the bruised and swollen body, he described to Alice the procedure about to be set in motion. But having explained, he was unable to resist returning to his part in the discovery.

'Not twenty feet away. If Harry hadn't taken the top off that rubbish then the chances are that I would have found her myself.' He sounded annoyed, somehow cheated.

Alice listened but didn't answer. She felt inexplicably relieved that the body had been discovered, that something, anything, had happened. It was, she thought, almost as if she had known what was going to happen, as if the murder had been in some indirect way connected with the way she had felt during the previous weeks. She felt now as she had felt on the night after visiting the theatre, the night she had walked away from the house along the Promenade with the wind and spray in her face and the sea drumming at the wall beneath her feet. She heard Norman but was not listening.

'That would have been something, eh?'

'It would, love. It would.' She did not ask him what he meant, but instead she turned and asked him if he remembered a holiday they had once spent in Torquay at a hotel with a real palm tree. There had been no honeymoon, only the holiday a year later, the palm tree not a yard from their window. She had leaned out and touched it, a towel fastened beneath her arms, the sun uncomfortably hot, Norman behind her, naked on the bed. She remembered everything – what he had said and done, and how he had looked. She wanted to talk about the holiday, but he remained with the girl's body, outlining the months ahead and already guessing at the outcome.

From outside came the sound of singing. A peal of bells sounded, and on either side of it the night seemed strangely silent. The light of the moon was reflected in a mirror. Alice watched it, remembering Torquay and waiting for something to happen, for the shadow of a cloud to block out the light. The singing grew louder and then faded.

Norman turned. 'Drunks. Just drunks.'

The silence was broken by a closing door and the sound of footsteps in the room above, the scrape of a chair.

The scarlet flare swung slowly from side to side, drawing a line of brilliant light through the darkness, its reflection rising to the surface of the sea to join it and disappear.

'Midnight,' Norman announced. 'Christmas Day. That's the flare from Danes End.' He looked towards the window, but saw nothing as the falling ball hit the water and sank.

Side by side, saying nothing, Norman and Alice looked up at the ceiling.

'Merry Christmas, love.'

'Yes, I suppose so.' And after a pause: 'We'll get him, you know. You can be sure of that.'

'Yes, love, of course you will.'

And for their different reasons both Alice and Norman smiled into the darkness.

Outside, a cat screamed like a new-born baby, something unseen and unsettling in the night.